THREADS OF FRIENDSHIP: Marge & Beth

Book 3 of The Bunco Club Series

Also by Karen DeWitt

The Bunco Club

Quilters of The Bunco Club: Phree & Rosa

THREADS OF FRIENDSHIP:
Marge & Beth

Book 3 of The Bunco Club Series

Karen DeWitt

Frame Masters, Ltd.
Matteson, Illinois 60443

Threads of Friendship: Marge & Beth

Cover by Karen DeWitt.

Published by Frame Masters, Ltd.
Matteson, Il 60443

ISBN-13: 978-0692375143 (Frame Masters, Ltd.)
ISBN-10: 0692375147

Printed in the United States of America.

To My Brother Bob DeWitt

Thank you for helping
my dreams become reality

List of Bunco Club Characters

Marge Russell: General Manager of the Mayflower Quilters Retreat, married (Bud), three children, control freak, quilter

Beth Stevenson: Salon owner/stylist, married (Tim), mother of three, hoarder, quilter

Phreedom (Phree) Clarke: Owner of the Mayflower Quilters Retreat, discovered valuable Mayflower documents, mother of Emily, divorced (Gary, aka The Bastard), quilter

Rosa Mitchell: Married (Terry), mother of Ricky and Alex, co-owner of The Pizza Depot with her husband, quilter

Lettie Peabody: Fiber artist, single woman, quilter

Nedra Lange: Social Media Guru at the Mayflower Quilters Retreat, widow (John), mother of two college age daughters, Executive Assistant to Editor-in-Chief at *Excel* Magazine, quilter

Helen Delaney: Married (Ben), mother of two, works at Quilter's Closet, quilter and long-arm quilter

Nancy Walsh: Single (boyfriend Michael), learning disabilities tutor, quilter

Sunnie Eaton: Mother of Phree Clarke Eaton, Assistant General Manager of The Mayflower Quilters Retreat

Brian Barber: Brother of Nedra Lange, lawyer

Chapter 1
September Bunco at Lettie's

Nightfall settled over the fields of suburban Chicago while a late September chill took on the appearance of fog creeping through rows of unharvested corn. Beth dodged potholes as she maneuvered her car over the familiar rutted lane that would take her to Lettie's farmhouse where the Bunco Club was meeting this month. With the Mayflower Quilters Retreat scheduled to open its doors next week by means of a 'soft opening,' the members of the Bunco Club had struggled to find an available evening that worked for all eight women *plus* the MQR's hectic timetable. Tonight was the best date that suited most of the group, so Beth had informed everyone that she'd have to arrive a little late on Bunco night.

The school's yearly open house had been held tonight at the Whitney Middle School where Beth and her husband pulled double-duty with their twins' eighth-grade teachers. Blessedly both Katy and Joey had gotten good reports. Even though Beth swore that the only thoughts going through Katy's head were cheerleading, boys, and being very very social, each teacher assured the Stevensons that their daughter's grades remained high.

Beth had felt a warm rush of pride when Mrs. McLean shared with her that Joey had recently aided an awkwardly shy sixth grader who had tripped in the hall. Apparently the child's books went sprawling along with the boy while his classmates stood by laughing and name-calling. Beth was aware that poor Jamie Balz had suffered for years with his surname as well as his weight, and she could only imagine the immature hilarity a group of prepubescent thirteen-and fourteen-year-olds could cook up over a dramatic tumble.

Mrs. McLean explained how Joey had disbanded the onlookers with a few brusque words and then helped Jamie gather his belongings. "I've seen this kind of compassionate leadership in Joey before," she said. "He's a good kid with a big heart and in my book that will take our boy a long way."

After parking her car next to Nancy's vehicle, Beth grabbed a hand-knit sweater from the backseat and stuffed the garment inside her tote bag that was already swollen with quilting show and tell. By the time the women would leave for home later tonight, she'd be happy for the light wrap to keep her warm. Entering Lettie's home as a late arrival, she found Bunco night in full swing. Still in 'open house mode' Beth felt a little disoriented for the first few moments. But with the melding aromas from the savory scent of food causing her tummy to complain, Beth's focus changed as she became sharply aware of her hunger.

"There she is!" called Rosa, as Beth placed her tote bag and purse near a pile of similar items that the women had formed around a wingback chair.

Lettie came forward to give her friend a welcoming hug. "Come load up your plate. I've kept everything warm for you. We've got a big pot of yummy Chicken Harvest Chowder Soup with three kinds of fresh homemade bread." Leaning in to stage-whisper she said, "I cheated on the homemade part of the bread and went straight to Panera's. But I guarantee the soup is made from scratch." Bringing her voice back to its normal range she added, "Help yourself to whatever you want...there's plenty."

"Let me tell you, everything's quite yummy," Marge said. "I wholeheartedly approve of tonight's menu."

"The soup is incredible," added Helen, "and perfect for this weather. Lettie's going to e-mail all of us the recipe tomorrow."

"How did the twins' open house go?" Nancy, an educator and learning disabilities tutor, asked Beth.

"I can't tell you how happy I am that the twins' last open house of grade school is finally behind us," Beth said. "And thank goodness we got two good reports. I'm still shocked that my wannabe cheerleader and social butterfly daughter is getting good grades." Beth spotted a candy dish filled with chocolate covered raisins and snagged a dozen or more of the sweet treat to take the edge off her hunger. "I would have been willing to bet the farm that she's only been going to school for social reasons...which basically means to see her boyfriend of the week."

All the women stepped aside so Beth could have her turn to feast on the bounty that Lettie had prepared for the evening's festivities.

"As usual, Lettie outdid herself." Nedra patted her flat tummy with slender hands that ended in perfectly manicured nails, but Beth knew that Nedra Lange was one of the biggest eaters in their group.

With a generous squeeze from salad tongs, crisp lettuce filled with chopped fresh vegetables landed next to a warm dollop of pizza dip on Beth's nearly full plate. "How the heck do you stay so thin?" Beth demanded of her friend. "I'm serious, Ned. I really want to know."

Nedra shrugged. "Good genes, I guess."

"Why don't you ask Ms. Good Genes about Mr. Hot-Middle-Aged-Construction-Guy?" Nancy said.

Nedra gaped, pretending to be appalled, and added with a head bobbing attitude, "His name is Nate and after you've quizzed me, don't forget to get the scoop on Nancy's Jeweler-Almost-Husband, the famous Michael Gibson."

Balancing a plate of food and a bowl of soup, Beth settled into a chair at one of the folding tables. Rosa walked through the room with a wine bottle wrapped in a towel refilling everyone's wineglass but didn't stop to offer any to Beth. After all these years everyone in the Bunco Club knew she didn't imbibe, and she was always thankful that none of her friends tried to coerce her. Asking a question to everyone, she said, "So, what did I miss by being late? Fill me in."

"Marge just started telling us a story," Phree said. "When we saw you driving down the lane, she decided to stop until you got here."

"I'm intrigued," Beth said and then bit into a thick slice of butter-slathered crusty bread.

"Well, there was no use in having to repeat myself and explain the ugly incident twice," Marge said and then added, "It's my sister again."

Several women moaned sympathetically while Phree said, "I assume you mean Laura."

Marge nodded her head. "Yeah, the youngest one."

"What kind of nutty thing did she do this time?" Rosa asked.

Marge settled into her chair to tell the latest 'crazy Laura story' but Beth saw sadness in her friend's eyes.

"She's just not a nice person…or a happy person," Marge said, shaking her head. "You all saw her at the baby shower a few weeks ago." Marge's eldest child, Jacob, had been born when she was only sixteen years old and her parents had forced her to put him up for adoption. A year ago bio-mom and child were reunited. This past month Marge hosted a meet-the-baby shower for little David, her first grandchild.

"I noticed she seemed a little off," Nedra shrugged. "I don't know…I guess you could say kind of cold."

"I'd say more like pissed off," Helen chimed in. "I tried to talk to her a few times until she finally blasted me with something along the lines of, 'I don't understand why I'm even here. I don't like kids and I can't stand babies. And here I am, trapped with a bunch of baby lovers.' Needless to say, I slithered away and left her alone after that."

Beth wasn't sure if it was out of frustration or

embarrassment that Marge exhaled loudly, squinted her eyes closed, and pinched the bridge of her nose. After opening her eyes she said, "You all know Laura and I have some bad blood. There have been years, especially when my kids were younger, that no matter how hard I tried she'd have nothing to do with my family. If she was involved with us for any reason, like around the holidays, we all walked on eggshells to keep her happy." Marge crossed her arms and rubbed her biceps as though warding off a chill. "We've only recently managed to eke out a civil two-way relationship. I truly hoped we had finally bridged the gap and that we might arrive at old age as the friends I had always wanted us to be."

"I understand completely," Nancy said. "Sisters can be difficult…I should know."

"With her history of mood swings, she's so darn unpredictable that I remained cautious. Recently I saw signs that she was sliding back into her hostile ways toward me so I figured it was just a matter of time before the other shoe dropped."

"Sounds like that shoe must have dropped pretty hard," Nedra said.

"Yeah. Apparently nothing's changed with her after all," Marge said sadly. "She called me about a week ago and reamed me good. I knew she had been stewing about something since the shower and the lid finally blew off. She gets so out of control, it's hard to explain and rather pathetic. If I'm being honest it's also a little scary how Laura can become riled up over absolutely nothing. She's so similar to Dad that it's like being belittled by him posthumously…assuming that he's dead by now."

"Huh?" Rosa looked confused. "I thought you told us your parents had both passed away."

"I've gotta say I'm pretty ashamed for having misled you all these years." Marge stared at her hands in her lap for a moment and then continued. "Whenever asked if they're still alive, I'm always careful to use the phrase: 'Mom and Dad are gone.' It's easier to default to that statement than go into an awkward explanation. People will come to their own conclusion and I don't have to expose an ugly secret. Anyway, in my heart I know Dad is dead."

Beth looked around the room. All movement had stopped. All eyes were on Marge.

"Long story short. When I was twenty-five years old our parents had an argument at a local bar…one of many, I might add. It was mid-February and Mom, as usual, had way too much to drink. She apparently told Dad she was going to the ladies room. Being drunk himself, he didn't realize how much time had elapsed. Who knows—maybe he assumed she was cooling off and chatting with someone else. Anyway, Mom probably thought she'd get even with him or piss him off even more and she decided to walk home." Marge paused. "It was eight degrees outside."

Several women moaned and Lettie said, "Oh, no."

"She fell. Probably hit her head, maybe passed out, we'll never know." Marge inhaled deeply and continued without much emotion. "By the time she was found Mom was suffering from severe frostbite and hypothermia. She died the next day."

"Why have we never heard this story before?" Nancy asked.

Shrugging, Marge said, "Telling secrets was like losing control for me. I guess I've learned a few things in this past year and started opening up more. Less secrets, more honesty is the new me."

Beth watched all the women nod their heads in understanding.

Continuing, Marge said, "Three years later, after Laura turned eighteen, Dad left home and never came back. We don't know how or when it happened, but the three of us girls are certain he's dead by now. I suspect at the very least his liver would have given out a long time ago."

"Wow, that's such a sad story," Phree said.

Helen reached over and placed a hand on Marge's arm. "I'm so sorry you had to go through that. You've sure had a rough time."

Waving them off, Marge said, "Thanks, but in the long run we're all better without either of them. I still sometimes play the 'what could have been' game when I think about Mom, but Dad was a poor excuse for a father. It was a good day for all of us when he disappeared."

Marge's hands went up in question. "So where was I before I got all honest on you?"

"Laura phoned and reamed you out." Nancy reminded her. "So what did she say?"

Marge nodded toward Helen. "Similar to what she said to Helen at the shower but nastier. She told me she was sick of my selfishness—her words—and that she would appreciate me not including her in any family matter that required her to bring money or a gift for my kids or grandchild."

Lettie's eyebrows rose as her lips formed a tight O shape.

Rosa reached to pat Marge's shoulder and said, "What a bitch."

Marge gulped the remainder of her wine and then placed the whole M&M dish on her lap. "Laura figures because she has no children that she's being taken advantage of by those of us who invite her to family parties for our kids."

Rosa asked, "What did you say?" Other than a few prompts like this, the women had remained quiet and listened attentively.

"I told her, 'Fine, I understand. I won't invite you anymore.' I think she was looking for a fight…some way to turn me into the bad person. So when I was somewhat polite and didn't argue with her, she hung up." Flopping her head onto the back of the chair, Marge stared at the ceiling for a moment. "Sisters can be so difficult. I can't stop dwelling on Laura. Why can't I be the kind of person that just says screw you? Why do I always think I need to fix everything? I wish I could forget about all the meanness she spews toward Jill and me." Marge put her fingers up to the side of her head and exploded her hand open. "Poof! Gone!"

"Sounds like a real challenge to be around her," Beth said.

"That's exactly what it is, Beth. It's a challenge; one where you always feel as though you're being tested, but that the right answer changes at the whim of an irrational person. I really can't begin to express how much Laura is like my dad." Marge bared her teeth and made a low growl in her throat. "Since I'm being all honest and introspective tonight, I have to say that my self-loathing was at an all-time high by the time I got to high school. Dad had chipped away at our dignity for years and had done quite a number both mentally and physically on the three of us girls…and Mom, too. Add to that he was a mean drunk and that beatings around the Parker home were the norm."

A chill slid down Beth's spine and she too was rubbing her upper arms for warmth. What her friend must have endured as a child was hard for Beth to comprehend. She had herself grown up in a home with loving parents and carefree siblings. Marge must have been one heck of a strong little girl, and Beth wondered what kind of woman Marge Russell would have been had she instead come from an adoring home.

"So, I refuse to sit back and allow anyone to demoralize me again. I'm more than ready to pull the plug on this flimsy relationship with my sister. It's simply too painful to have her in my life never knowing when the next unreasonable explosion will take place." Marge slapped her hands on her knees. "Well, that got awful heavy. Can you tell I can't get this Laura thing out of my head? Enough of my dysfunctional story. Sorry if it sounds like I'm throwing a pity party, ladies, but thanks for listening. I needed to vent."

In an obvious attempt to change the subject, Marge looked toward Beth and said, "I think Helen has some news for you."

Helen's eyes went bright. "Weelll…" She drew out the word to two syllables adding suspense. "My longarm quilting machine, better known as Lilly Marie, has been busy. I have your two tops quilted and I brought them along for you tonight."

Beth butt-hopped up and down on the seat of the chair and patted her hands together. "Oh, I can't wait to see them! Please tell me I don't have to wait until after we play Bunco for show and tell."

"Yes, ma'am," Helen said. "Just like everyone else."

Beth smiled, dabbed at her lips with a napkin, and said, "As long as no one else has seen their finished quilts, then I guess I can wait too." But what she really wanted to say was more along the lines of, *Wait till the end of the night? Are you crazy? I want to see them right now!*

"I've already told the others this little tidbit before you arrived," Rosa said, "so I'll keep my tale short and sweet. That hideous tattoo on Ricky's thumb is officially gone. Laser." She knifed her hand through the air like a hatchet. "Kaput."

"Seriously?" Beth was surprised but shouldn't have been. After all, who wants their child going through life with the 'F' word permanently inked on a thumb? "How'd he take it?" she asked.

"Oh, he wanted that thing gone as much as Terry and I did. Removing a tattoo by laser hurts like hell—worse than getting the original tat. Terry went with him…I just couldn't."

"Is he doing okay?" Beth asked.

"He's doing really well…I'm so darn proud of him." Rosa placed a hand over her heart. "Ricky still has a long way to go to fully recover from this mess but I'm confident he'll eventually pull through. As a matter of fact, you'll see him next week at the retreat. He's working opening day and he'll also be coming after school most of the week." Rosa laughed.

"I think he's having as much fun at the retreat as the rest of us. The food alone that the head chef has been shoveling into him would be enough enticement for any teenage boy."

Phree slipped up behind Rosa and put an arm around her shoulder. "We all love having Ricky at the retreat. He's managing quite well and he's fun to have around. He's got his mother's vivacious personality."

Rosa's hair went wild as she shook her head and threw her hands in the air like a television preacher and said, "God forbid!"

With only six days until the retreat opened its doors, Beth didn't want to be left out of the loop. "Did I miss any MQR talk?"

"No," Phree said. "We were waiting for you before we start on the subject."

Marge looked nervous as she glanced toward the clock on the DVD player. "I don't know, ladies. It's getting pretty late. Maybe we should play Bunco first and talk about the retreat over dessert."

"No way!" Rosa said. "Dump the timetable, Captain Marge. We all want info on what's going on over there."

"From my point of view," Phree said, "I think we're in great shape. Wouldn't you say everything is under control, Marge?"

"I'm confident we'll be ready to roll on Sunday when our first guests arrive." Marge spoke with authority as she slipped into her role of general manager. "Nate and Josh are the dream team of contractors. They're pushing their crew to complete the detailed finishing touches by Wednesday and then a cleaning service is scheduled to come in on Thursday to give the whole retreat a thorough once-over."

"I, for one, can't wait to get rid of all of the nasty construction dust," Phree interjected as she waved a hand in front of her face and crumpled her nose.

"Friday is earmarked for housekeeping to do their

magic," Marge continued. "I'll snag a small team of workers to help me set up the sitting and visiting areas. I want to optimize those spaces for hand sewing and talking."

"I'm looking forward to seeing all of that gorgeous furniture without plastic tarps draped all over it," Nedra said. "That'll be the first day of my ten days off work so I'll be on-site to capture the transformation on camera. I think it will make for a cool blog post."

"Great idea," Beth said.

"Of course the Galley won't be part of this final cleaning binge since Chef Evelyn's crew has been preparing and stocking the kitchen for the past few weeks. She's run some of her menu ideas past us with mini-tastings and, allow me to say, the guests are in for one taste sensation after another."

Rosa hmmphed and crossed her arms over her chest. "Why weren't any of us invited to these mini-tastings?"

"Spur of the moment," Marge said. "Truly, Rosa, completely spontaneous. Evelyn would stick her head inside the office door at any given moment and say, 'You ladies got a minute?' "

"And of course not wanting to disappoint our new head chef," Phree laughed, "we crawled all over each other to get to the dining room first. She often summoned us as many as four times a day. It was a tough job but Marge, Sunnie, and I performed our duties admirably." Phree bowed.

"I heard from Nate that he was on dessert detail," Nedra said.

"Once Chef Evelyn caught wind that the head contractor had a sweet tooth, he was presented with his own work-site treats," Marge explained. "All he had to do was say 'yay or nay' and the goodies just kept coming. Evelyn would send a kitchen worker in a white chef jacket looking for Nate with orders to get his input. She carried a single cookie or slice of pie or whatever on a china plate covered by a white linen napkin through the whole retreat until she located him. Then she stood waiting for his reply like one of those Western Union boys from the old movies."

"If I'm not mistaken he gave his approval to everything he tasted, but I heard the scones were his favorite. 'The best I've ever had. Melt in your mouth,' was what he told me." Nedra looked toward Helen, the Bunco Club's very own Scone Queen. "Sorry, Helen, I'm sure he'd love your scones just as much if he ever tried them...I mean…"

Helen smiled, and raised her hands in a 'no problem' gesture.

"Evelyn is using Helen's recipe," Marge informed the group. "She was nice enough to share."

"Consider the scone recipe as my contribution to the success of the MQR," Helen replied.

"Any chance scones will be on the menu for every meal?" Nancy laughed. "Because if they are, I think I'm moving in."

With another check of the DVD's clock Marge said, "Okay, ladies. Let's move along smartly and get this game going."

Rosa objected like a spoiled child and whined, "But what if we don't want to? Maybe I want to keep talking."

"Tough," Lettie said. "Get your butt over here, Mitchell, and stop complaining."

And of course Rosa, ever the mature one of the group, tilted her head and stuck out her tongue at tonight's hostess.

Once again Marge flattened her palms on her thighs and pushed to stand up. "Now, if Rosa is done being childish, I've got one final reminder for everyone. Thursday of next week is our Meet-the-People-Behind-the-Retreat Dinner. If at all possible you're welcome to come early and visit with the guests and talk amongst them, or talk about quilting or stitching, books, recipes, children, whatever you want. Try to get an idea how they felt about their week at the retreat." Marge threw her hands out in front of her. "Heck, if you'd like, feel free to bring some handwork and join in with some of the stitchers. It doesn't need to be said but I will say it anyway: keep all visiting friendly and casual."

As the women moved into place at the two card tables, Helen said to Nedra, "What's going on with Nate?"

"We manage to eke out some time to occasionally get together," Nedra answered.

"Oh come on," Rosa whined. "It's more difficult to get information out of you than it is getting money from a slot machine. When are you going to fill us in on Mr. Perfect?"

"When there's something to tell."

"Well," Lettie said, "if the romance falls through with Nate, don't forget about Eric from little David's baby shower. I watched how he followed you around that day with his tongue hanging out."

"Enough!" Nedra cried, but Beth watched her friend laughing and knew she was enjoying the good-natured taunts. "Please make them start playing Bunco, Marge. It's getting awfully late."

"Ladies, I'm afraid Ned's correct. The clock is ticking and we must begin. But first things first…we're not doing a thing until Nedra tells us if she is indeed dating two men at once."

"Oh, for goodness sakes, of course I'm not! At least not anymore."

A round of whoops and wolf whistles erupted.

"Put those dice down, Ms. Lange, and explain yourself," Beth commanded, as her friend covered her face with both hands and began shaking her head.

"Okay, okay." Nedra uncovered her face. "I went out with Eric three times but my heart wasn't in it. Every time we were together I wanted to be with Nate. That's all." Nedra made a show of pounding her fist on the table. "Now no more pumping for information."

Phree, who had grown close to Nedra during the Mayflower discovery last year, leaned over the table and in a loud whisper said to everyone, "Don't worry, ladies, I'll get the info out of her and then I'll fill you in on the scoop."

Shaking her head as though to clear away the madness, Nedra rolled her eyes heavenward and said, "Let's play Bunco, you gossiping hens."

Lettie poured another round of wine as the women seated themselves at the two card tables. Rosa continued the interrogation of Nedra until she was convinced that their friend was not going to come clean with any new details about her love life. Someone rang the handheld bell to start the game and the dice began to roll. For the remainder of the evening the talking, eating, and laughing never ceased.

As usual, another late night was on tap for the women of the Bunco Club.

Chapter 2
Marge

The clock would take another five to six minutes before the sun crested over the thinning tree tops behind Marge who had, of course, organized the beginning of this momentous day so even the sunlight was required to cooperate with her plans. Backing her car into a spot at the far end of the Mayflower Quilters Retreat parking lot she would view the fleeting image that was about to reveal itself. Placing her SUV in park she noticed Phree, the owner of the MQR, must still be asleep. Her home behind the retreat, referred to as the Crow's Nest, was devoid of any lamplight. Walled in by the shadowy forest surroundings, Phree's home was mostly hidden.

As the general manager of the quilters retreat, once Marge opened her car door, the day would begin in earnest. Many long hours would pass before she was able to afford the luxury of another quiet moment to herself.

Surrounded by predawn darkness, Marge felt for the folded piece of paper in the back pocket of her jeans. She had awakened this morning to an e-mail from her sister. Scanning the words on her computer screen, she had experienced the combined emotions of sorrow, exhaustion with the never ending no-win mind games that Laura played, and a heaping portion of anger. *Who does she think she is and how dare she!* Marge had clicked the print button, folded the paper to fit in her pocket, and vowed *this* time she would not dwell on the craziness.

She would never allow others to treat her this way, so why had she always made exceptions for her sibling? Laura had manipulated Marge into feeling horrible for the last time. She would end her partnership in the sadistic dance of the Parker sisters. The victim would not forgive the wrongdoer this time; instead she would hold the perpetrator responsible for her rudeness and her actions.

No time would exist in today's busy schedule for pondering this familial dilemma, and feeling the crinkle of paper through the jeans material would be a reminder that Laura had put her meanness in writing this time...to be revisited by Marge as often as needed. She was hopeful there might be a few minutes to share some of her concerns about her sister with Sunnie.

In the rearview mirror the morning sky had lightened in a matter of seconds from inky ebony to soft gray flannel. Sprinkles of peach and streaks of rose appeared while nudging the dark night aside until at 6:43 a.m. the arc of the sun crept over the horizon line of the forest. Inching into position, brightness spilled through leafless branches of the tallest trees to rest on the oversized Friendship Star quilt block which had been hand painted on the east end of the MQR building to welcome visitors. The soft blue colors, which had been chosen to embody the comfort and friendliness of the retreat, glowed in the morning light and contrasted with its natural surroundings—the perfect 'pop' of color to make the painted quilt block sing.

Today marked the culmination of months of hard work, and a select amount of quilters were due to arrive between the hours of noon and three p.m. to participate in the official 'soft opening' of the Mayflower Quilters Retreat. Enjoying the vision before her, coupled with the late-in-life career change she had recently made, Marge delighted in the chatter of birds as they also began their day. With only five hours before the first quilter would check in, she flipped the handle on the car door, leaned to push it open, and said under her breath, "Time to get the show on the road."

Unlocking the door triggered a piercing blast from the first floor security system in the retreat. After tapping in the code to unarm the noisy device, Marge deposited an armload of items on her desk and then turned on the screens for the surveillance cameras. Eager to make a quick inspection throughout the rooms of the MQR before anyone arrived, she headed down the hall. Her footfalls echoed through the emptiness while she scrutinized every inch of the building, taking mental notes on anything that needed attention. She didn't find many issues beyond a few semidry flower pots that needed watering and several long tables in the sewing area that she nudged into their proper place by inches. For the past two days the staff had fine-tuned every last detail for the opening, and Marge was close to making the executive call to proceed at full speed ahead.

As the elevator door opened on the second floor, the scent of freshly brewed coffee wafted toward her. Phree's mother, Sunnie, must be awake and preparing for the day. Sunnie, the Assistant GM of the retreat, worked hand-in-hand with Marge and lived on-site in one of the four suites. She would be in charge and available throughout the nighttime and during any other intervals that Marge was not on the premises.

Weaving in and out of every room in the sleeping quarters, the astute GM kept an eye toward perfection and consistency. Everything looked to be in place. Each room sported two new twin beds with their own nightstands; two rooms were connected by a shared bathroom. On Sunnie's suggestion, secondhand dressers had been purchased from thrift stores and garage sales and had been individually painted and creatively embellished to add uniqueness and charm to what could have otherwise easily become sterile-looking identical rooms. The individual styles of the colorful dressers reminded Marge of a teatime table setting displaying an eclectic mix of china cups and saucers.

Housekeeping had done a thorough job preparing the rooms, and Marge scrawled a note on her tablet reminding herself to compliment the crew on a job well done. Later this morning fresh flowers would be delivered from a local florist for the dining room, foyer, all the bedrooms, and other miscellaneous spots throughout the building. At the opposite end of the hallway from the elevator, the finicky GM took the stairs down to the first floor. With the tour complete, Marge was delighted that the MQR had passed her meticulous white-glove test and in so doing had earned her personal stamp of approval.

Late yesterday afternoon, per Marge's directions and diagram sketched on graph paper, maintenance had carefully set up tables in the spacious foyer for what would be the check-in area. Wanting to make a good first impression with their guests or passengers, Marge had chosen soft pastel quilts to adorn the check-in tables. Before leaving the retreat last night Marge had dressed the tables, smoothing the quilts out flat with the palms of her hands to prevent any unsightly wrinkles.

Placing the finishing touches on the check-in area, Marge was attaching custom-made quilted name tags to the swag bags they would distribute to their guests when Sunnie approached the table.

"Morning, Marge. You ready for today? What can I do to help?"

Marge stood up straight and arched her back into a stretch as she spoke. "Thanks for the offer, but I think we're done here." Gathering the bits and pieces of ribbons and raffia left over from the name tags, she added, "Actually, I think we're in pretty good shape overall. Why don't you join me in the office for a cuppa while we wait for the others to arrive?"

The board members, who were the eight women from the Bunco Club along with Phree's mother, Sunnie, were scheduled to convene in the conference room at nine a.m. for a private meeting and 'game day' pep rally. Joining her arm with Marge's, Sunnie said, "Good idea, hon. Let's caffeine up before the big day starts. Any sign of my daughter yet?"

A small laugh escaped Marge as she answered, "No." Extending her arm in front of her to indicate the entire building before them, she stage-whispered to Sunnie, "I think Phree is the only one of us who *isn't* nervous about the opening."

"I know what you mean. She seems completely unaffected by all of this." In her early sixties, Sunnie usually dressed in a pair of tattered jeans, wearing a deconstructed or recycled top of her own creation. Birdlike thin with a short pixie-style haircut and the tiniest diamond stud in her nose, Phree's mother was anything but an invisible senior. "I popped my head in the kitchen a few minutes ago to see how things were going. Evelyn was smiling her brains out and excited to get this first day under her belt. The rest of the team looked equally happy and enthusiastic."

"I like hearing that." Picking up a stack of manila folders and adding a yellow-lined tablet on top, Marge grasped them in her arm and said, "The others should start arriving any minute. Let's head to the conference room and prepare for a whirlwind board meeting."

The Mayflower Quilters Retreat had come about after Phree had discovered near priceless documents from her Mayflower ancestors in an old trunk that had been unknowingly passed down through her family. She then purchased an expanse of property that included a complex of empty buildings which had once been a nunnery. The main building had oodles of space, was renovated rather quickly, and had been masterfully converted into a state-of-the-art quilters haven.

In a corner of the conference room an oversized tea cart stood where Sunnie arranged a small porcelain basket of tea bags, several varieties of K-cups, and mugs sporting the MQR logo. Marge organized her files and wrote a few last-minute notes. Evelyn, the head chef, entered the room and placed a tray of heavenly smelling, freshly baked and still-warm-from-the-oven cookies near the coffee maker.

"Good luck today, ladies," she said to the GMs.

"Same to you," Marge replied. "Keep me posted throughout the day, especially if there are any problems in the kitchen or dining room."

Phree was the first to arrive and entered the room saying, "Can you believe it's finally our first day? On one hand it feels like the time just flew by getting to this point, but on the other hand it seems as though it's taken forever." She walked to her mother and kissed her cheek. "Hi, Mom. Are you guys ready for this?"

"You bet we are." Sunnie delivered a quick embrace to her daughter. "And I wouldn't want to be anywhere but right here beside you."

Nedra came through the door next, with Helen and Beth close behind. All three were laughing about something.

"Get yourselves some coffee and cookies and take a seat, ladies," Marge said. "I want to keep this meeting brief. Does anyone know if Rosa was going to be late for any reason?"

Rosa was perpetually late for everything.

"Lettie told me she was picking her up to make sure Rosa," Nedra made air quotes with her fingers, "got her butt here on time."

"Did I hear my name?" Rosa entered the room with a full tote bag and Lettie following behind. "I would have been here sooner but Miss Small-Bladder," she pointed with her thumb over her shoulder, "couldn't hold it for five more minutes till we got here. We had to stop at McDonald's for a potty break."

Lettie looked embarrassed and a little frazzled but said, "Oh, stop complaining, Rosa. I got you here with a minute to spare," her eyes scanned the room. "And it actually looks like you aren't last to arrive for a change."

Marge looked toward the women, and then pointed at each item as she said, "Coffee. Cookies. Chair."

Rosa saluted. "Aye aye, Captain." Marge had gone from being called Marge the Sarge by the group to Captain, as in Captain of the Mayflower.

Marge closed her eyes and exhaled a long breath through tight lips, but was saved from saying something she might regret when Nancy entered the room.

"Sorry, Marge. It looks like I'm the last one here but it's exactly nine o'clock by my phone so technically I'm not late."

"That's fine, Nancy. We'll get started while you get yourself some refreshments." Marge turned her attention to the head of the long table. "Would you please open the meeting, Phree?"

As President of the Board, Phree did what was necessary to be both official and legal to get the Mayflower Quilters Retreat board meeting started. "I personally want to thank everyone." She extended her arms, bent at the elbows in front of her and gently clapped her hands while nodding at her friends. "For all that you have done to help bring the MQR to this momentous point. It's our big day, so let's make some quilty memories for our passengers this week and let's remember to have fun while we're doing it." The other women applauded lightly and Phree said, "That's all I got. I'm handing the meeting over to our GM and fearless Captain, Marge Russell."

"As I said, I want to keep this meeting as brief as possible." The GM glanced at the clock above the coffee maker. "Within three hours our first guests will start to arrive, and we still have a lot of work to do." Marge passed a stack of copies with the day's agenda to her left and they continued around the long oak table until each woman had one. "We'll be fully staffed in the kitchen as we would any day the retreat is open. Maintenance will be up and running during the daytime hours of seven a.m. to seven p.m. and then there will be someone on call from seven in the evening to seven in the morning for emergencies. Any problems with sinks, toilets, doors, electrical..." Marge placed her hands palms up in front of her and said, "*Anything* building related...goes through maintenance first."

Looking up, Marge smiled at Rosa. "Our boy Ricky will be getting here about eleven thirty this morning and will stay with us through dinner. He'll be helping the guests schlepp their belongings into the retreat, up to their rooms, and to the quilting area. Ricky will also be lending a hand anywhere else he might be needed and then in the kitchen around mealtime." Marge directed her next comment to Rosa, yet it was said for all to hear. "Ricky was a big help to us this summer, and we're happy to have him on board whenever he can make it now that school has started."

Rosa gave the thumbs-up signal along with a wide smile, indicating that her son was doing well since his return home.

Marge referred to her notes to find her place. "Due to the fact that the participants of this retreat are comprised of quilters from local guilds or shops who registered in our online giveaway contest for a free spot in the soft opening, there won't be any shuttles running to the airports this week." Flipping to a chart on the next page of notes, she took an extended breath.

"Now, for our assignments today..." Marge looked toward Phree. "Phree will introduce herself and welcome guests on the porch before they enter the building. If a line of passengers has not formed, I think it would be a nice gesture if you would individually escort the women inside. I'll be at the check-in table with Rosa." Marge made eye contact with each woman as she mentioned their names. "Helen, you'll pull double-duty by directing guests to the various rooms on the first floor while also overseeing the quilt and necessities shop. There's bound to be a flurry of forgotten items on the first day—both sewing related and personal—so I suspect there could be a number of visitors to the Ship's Store.

"I'd like Nancy and Beth to help the women select a station and get settled in the Hannah Brewster Quilting Room. Two things, Beth…I have a quick tour of the Pampered Pilgrim Salon scheduled for you at four o'clock this afternoon so any interested guests can take a peek. Also a box of supplies was delivered for the salon yesterday. The package is still in my office so maybe you can take care of it before noon when the quilters start arriving."

Beth nodded. "I'll check into it as soon as the meeting's over."

"As the MQR historian and media guru," Marge continued, "Nedra will be taking photos all day for our social media sites and blog. She will also be 'on call' for any scheduled or surprise media visits. Sunnie and Lettie will act as floaters and fill in wherever needed. If there are any questions you can't answer or problems you need help with, hunt us down or text us and we'll get right on it. We'll be close-by at all times. Are there any questions?"

There were none.

"I'm going to turn the floor over to Nedra to explain what is planned as far as media coverage for this week."

Nedra folded her hands in front of her and with the graceful self-confidence of a TV anchorwoman enlightened the board members about upcoming events. "Normally, media coverage for the opening of a quilters retreat would garner very little, if any, media attention…but, luckily for the MQR, Phree became an instant celebrity with her Mayflower discovery last fall." Nedra pointed her hand toward their friend, and Phree nodded her head in recognition. "Further good news is that the whole country is fascinated with and can't seem to get enough of Ms. Phree Clarke Eaton."

Phree laughed. "I know. Hard to believe isn't it?"

"So, the long and the short of it is that throughout this week we not only have the five local TV channels coming out here to film what the Mayflower Quilters Retreat is all about, but two of the cable biggies will visit as well. Of course I'll be writing the piece for *Excel*, and we're in the process of negotiating a time slot when *People* magazine will send someone out. Several Chicagoland newspapers will also be doing feature articles on the retreat, and two quilting magazines are very enthusiastic about covering the story."

There were oohs and ahs from the table of friends, and Helen said, "That's got to be great for business, Phree."

"You bet it is," Nedra replied. "Per my brother Brian, each guest will sign a release stating that they agree to be photographed, filmed, televised, and possibly used in future advertising." Nedra passed several sheets of paper to Marge. "This is the temporary schedule that I have in place so far. It's very fluid, but I'll keep Marge updated on any changes or additions."

"Man, this is impressive," Beth said. "All I can say is thank God you're in the industry and know what the heck you're doing."

"Well, don't oversell me. I'm just in the print media. This is a whole new area for me. I'm really learning as I go, but at least I understand the terminology when something technical is mentioned." Nedra put her hands out, palms up. "And that's it for me. Back to Marge."

"Don't sell yourself short," Marge said. "I can only presume that having Nedra Lange as the contact person for interviews didn't hurt when the media came snooping around."

The door to the boardroom opened and the head of housekeeping said, "Sorry to disturb you, Marge, but you asked me to let you know when floral got here. They just rolled up."

"Thanks, Judy, I'll be right there." Marge looked to Phree and stood. "Shall we close the meeting? But first are there any questions?"

"Yes, I have one," Lettie said. "I think we all want to know if there's any news on Baby David since Bunco last week. How is he?"

Sitting down, Marge said, "I'll give you the condensed version for now. As you all know they let my grandson go home last month after getting the 'all clear' from the hospital, but Jacob and Niesha are understandably still very nervous and concerned. I really don't blame them. They had the life scared out of them. Having meconium aspiration in a newborn is very scary. While blessedly David's prognosis is excellent, I think right now his parents need a little time to heal from the experience."

"Thank God he'll be okay," Nancy said. "I'm glad for your sake that we were able to fit in the postponed shower before the retreat opened."

"Thanks for asking after David." Marge paused and smiled. "Now, let's move along smartly and finish with the preliminaries before our guests arrive."

"I move to adjourn the meeting," said Helen.

Marge already started to stand as she said, "And I'll second the motion."

Phree smacked the gavel once on the sound block to make it official.

Chapter 3
Beth

"I'll be in the Pampered Pilgrim if anyone needs me," Beth called above the din of excited chatting voices as the women exited the conference room.

"The Pampered Pilgrim sounds like a swanky nightclub or maybe a strip joint," Rosa laughed. "Need any help over there?"

"Nah, I've got it, but thanks."

"One last thing, ladies." Marge rapped her knuckles on the table and raised her voice to be heard. "Don't forget to store your purses in my office in the employee closet. They'll be safe there. No need to be carrying them around with you all day."

A shared eye-roll between Rosa and Beth didn't need any words.

The Pampered Pilgrim was located at the far end of the retreat past the kitchen in what used to be the live-in cook's rooms. The genius of the head contractor, who had spearheaded the remodel of the old convent into a quilter's haven, had miraculously converted the cook's rooms into an efficient and inviting mini-salon/spa. Setting the box of new supplies on the floor in front of the door, Beth punched in the key code. There were very few rooms that were locked at the MQR but the salon was one of them and Beth had wholeheartedly agreed with the decision.

Having helped with the design of the one-chair shop, it was like entering a 'dream salon' for Beth; everything was brand new and perfectly organized. Lacking a single spritz of hair spray or an open bottle of nail polish, the space smelled wonderfully fresh and new. Thinking she might enjoy the solitude back here for a while, Beth would take her time opening the box and shelving the new inventory. Fishing out several cans of hair spray and mousse, along with bottles and jars of various products from the cardboard carton, Beth couldn't help but admire the heavy-duty box which was filled with thin crinkly ribbons of thick brown paper. She knew the container would be sturdy for shipping as well as handy for storing fragile items. She would hang on to this treasure that most people would overlook, tucking it someplace safe away from prying eyes and judgmental comments. Reuse. Recycle. Never throw away.

This past February, after her widowed father had moved into an active retirement community, Beth had some newfound time on her hands. She made a noble effort to purge the Stevensons' home of the overwhelming clutter and disorder the family had lived with for far too long. However, when it came time to actually dispose of vast piles and mounds of varied items, Beth found herself confused and anxious. It was at that point when she chose to deftly consolidate items from jumbled heaps into a tightly organized 'private collection' in large plastic bins. Shuffling and shifting the bins into place in the family's previously knee-deep-with-junk basement had been a temporary fix—one that looked great but could easily turn ugly *if* or *when* her hubby prodded around seeking a misplaced item. Beth was aware that she needed to take action to avoid that. But what to do? She had no idea...not one single thought.

Coming close to a mini - panic attack over her ever-growing guilt was not an option on this busy day. Manipulating the flaps of the open box until she had them flipped over each other and locked into place, Beth opened the exit door of the salon to the brilliant skies of a warm fall day. The fresh air and short walk to her parked car did wonders to soothe the frayed edges of her guilt. As she took a shortcut across the grass to the extended parking lot which had been added for employees, she noted that the birdsong had recently taken on a tune of impending migration. Safely stowing her newest treasure next to several items she had picked up at a garage sale earlier this morning on her way to the MQR, Beth could now push her worries to the back of her mind and focus on the thrill of being part of this amazing retreat.

On the short stroll back to the Pampered Pilgrim's exit door, Beth attempted to keep calm, but for some reason squirreling away that cardboard box had triggered a mountain of shameful feelings. And lately, each time she became uncomfortable with what she was doing, it was more and more difficult to convince herself that she had nothing to feel bad about.

She remembered the mantra she recited as she sorted box after box of objects during that cold winter month ... *Do I want* you *or do I want my family?* It could never really come to that, could it...being forced to choose?

The only way to avoid the desperation and chest-tightening anxiety she faced on trash day was a knee-jerk reaction: Never put anything potentially useful, personal, or emotional in the garbage...but therein lay the problem. Everything was potentially useful, personal, or emotional when viewed through Beth's possessive eyes. *Remember,* she told herself as she secured the salon door from the inside, *this is not the time or the place to figure out the dynamics of this personal quandary.*

The first guests would be arriving at the retreat soon, and Beth wanted to be able to play her part with confidence and cheer. These stressful scenarios that had been replaying themselves in her head needed to stop. After all, she wasn't doing anything wrong and she really did have everything under control.

Approaching the foyer and check-in area Beth could

hear her friends talking and laughing in the large domed space. It was only twenty-five minutes until the first guest might possibly arrive—check-in was noon till three p.m. She lingered in the doorway for a moment soaking in the sight of all her dear friends together and excited. They were all wearing the required color-of-the-day Mayflower Quilters Retreat polo shirt—today was Sunday and that meant pink shirts with dark-gray lettering.

At the check-in table sat Marge, head down and thumbing through a pile of papers, most likely reorganizing her already organized, numerical, and alphabetized stack of handouts. Rosa relaxed in the copilot seat next to Marge where she was not at all concerned about paperwork or check-in details. Her son Ricky leaned against the wall and talked with his mother and Lettie. At one point he folded his arms, bent his knee, and placed his oversized gym shoe on the wall behind him. Before the sole of the shoe had a moment to rest on the pristine wall, Rosa swatted at his leg and frowned while nodding her head sideways at Marge…in mother-speak, 'Get your foot off the wall and don't let *her* see you do that!' Ricky snapped his foot away from the wall and looked embarrassed, but Rosa patted his leg and Beth read her lips, "It's okay. No problem, honey."

Nedra stood by the oversized niche in the curved wall that held a remarkably beautiful floral arrangement. A fancy camera dangled from a strap around her neck, and she was fussing with the buttons of a much smaller model camera. The rest of the group was off to the side intently listening to Sunnie talking. All the women were smiling, and Nancy had her hand covering her mouth, as if to hold back a reaction. Suddenly the whole group hooted with laughter as Sunnie shrugged her shoulders with an I-don't-get-it shake to her head.

Beth took in the scene within a matter of seconds and started over to the knot of women recovering from Sunnie's story. Movement outside caught her eye and she hustled over to the group informing Phree. "Oh, my God, I think a guest is here," she hissed loud enough for all the women in the tight group to hear. For a fragment of a second Beth watched as Phree's eyes went wild while she paled ever so slightly. Then her friend inhaled a long breath, turned on her heel, and headed toward the door saying, "It's show time."

All the women and Ricky Mitchell became aware that the Big Moment had arrived as Nedra rushed forward to digitally record this important moment forever.

Chapter 4
Marge

Snapping her eyes toward the main entrance, Marge felt her stomach slam toward her throat. Phree was greeting their first guest and briefly chatting with her as Marge loud-whispered, "Ladies, to your posts. Move along smartly!" She didn't have to tell them twice. Each woman shot out of the foyer as though a stretched rubber band had been connected to them and had just let go. Ricky, sporting a navy-blue MQR polo with khaki pants, stepped across the threshold and into the bright autumn sunshine, where he remained a comfortable distance from Phree and the guest.

Marge couldn't see Phree from her vantage point but heard her say, "This is Rick, and he'll help with your belongings if you'd like." It sounded odd to hear Rosa's son called by his more 'adult' name of Rick—especially when their group still referred to him as Ricky.

"Oh, that would be wonderful. Thank you, Rick."

Marge could tell from the voice this was a slightly older woman.

"I still have mounds of things that need to be brought in. I wondered how I was going to manage it all."

"No worries, ma'am." Ricky relieved the woman of her rolling suitcase. "I have a large handcart that should get everything inside with one trip. As soon as I know your room assignment, I'll bring this luggage up for you. When you're ready to have me bring in your other items, just let me know."

"Flawless," Marge thought. *"Exactly as we practiced."*

The woman approached the check-in table and Marge

greeted her with a cheery hello. "My name is Marge. Welcome aboard the Mayflower Quilters Retreat."

"I really and truly *never* win anything and I was shocked when my name was drawn to attend this week." The woman fluttered a hand in front of her face and said, "Oh, I am so excited to be here."

"And we're excited to have you join us. What's your name please?"

Nedra clicked the camera from several angles as Marge and the first guest, Shirley Gaines, completed the brief registration procedure. Marge passed the swag bag and pocket folder of handouts to the pleasant woman. There was a floor plan of the first floor on top of the folder that Marge pointed to, as she noticed that Ricky—eh Rick—was already back from depositing the first guest's luggage in room number five, the Sawtooth Star Room. She also heard Phree greeting someone else, and it was only eleven forty-five!

Marge stood, smiled at this pleasant lady, and pointed. "If you go that way, you'll see the elevator and a large stairway. Take whichever one you prefer."

After Shirley thanked Marge for her help, Rick said to their guest, "Whenever you're ready for your belongings just let me know."

"Oh, I will, dear." Shirley introduced herself to Rosa and said, "What a nice young man."

Marge knew that was all it would take for Rosa to strike up not only a conversation but a friendship with this woman. Straightening the already straight papers, she prepared for the second guest when she heard a raised voice from the porch say, "Well, how do I know he's trustworthy?"

"I've known Rick my whole life. His mother is one of my best friends and sits on my board of directors." Marge could tell by her voice that Phree was riled. "You're perfectly welcome to bring your own belongings inside if you prefer."

"Why would I want to do that? Here are my car keys

but don't even think of taking my car for a joyride, young man. Bring those keys right back to me after everything is delivered to the proper places."

In a clipped voice Phree said, "This is how we do things at the MQR," and proceeded to tell the new guest that Rick would transport her sewing items to the sewing area and leave them stacked in one spot. The guest was responsible for claiming and setting up her own sewing station. If she needed further help with getting luggage upstairs, she could ask Rick and he would get to it when he had time.

This exchange only took a matter of minutes. Marge was happy that Rosa was still occupied chatting with Shirley, or she would have feared what Ricky's mother might do to this rude woman. Splashing a welcoming but fake smile on her face, Marge greeted the next guest, who interrupted her before she could finish.

"I didn't realize you allowed early-bird check-ins." The woman spoke so loudly that Rosa and Shirley stopped talking.

"We frown on it, but we're happy to check you in." Marge was being as smiley sweet as she could.

"I'm not talking about *me*...obviously you'll check me in since you already checked in that one." She nodded her head sideways toward Shirley.

"Oh, dear." Shirley reddened. "I do apologize if I broke a rule."

"Next time look at your watch, Grandma," the disgruntled guest said.

Marge heard Rosa suck in her breath and when she stood up quickly, Marge was ready to place a restraining hand on her friend's arm. Instead, Rosa said, "Come with me, Shirley." And to Helen who was standing nearby, "Would you be so kind as to ask Sunnie to meet us in the dining room, please?" Rosa linked arms with Shirley. "As our very first guest ever to the MQR, we have a little surprise for you."

"We do? Really? Crap! This is only our second guest and I've already lost control," Marge thought.

The rude guest looked around and called out, "Who's in charge here?"

"I am," Marge said with lips tight. "I am the General Manager of the Mayflower Quilters Retreat."

"Let me just tell you that I'm not happy right now. I fully intended to be the first guest to this retreat and was waiting patiently in my car until I could line up at the door at the appropriate time."

"This woman is nasty," thought Marge.

"You can imagine my surprise when the owner of this place told me that even though it wasn't officially time yet, I could check in because somebody already had! Now I find that I lost out on the big surprise the first guest is entitled to."

Exhaling her frustration, Marge simply said, "May I have your name, please?"

"No need to sigh at me, Marge Russell. My name is Heloise Simmons. That's Heloise with an H," she sniffed.

Marge was tempted to inform Heloise-with-an-H that there must be some mistake—that she couldn't possibly have won a free week here because her name was *not* on their list of winners, but instead she said, "You'll have to sign this media release, please." Marge pointed to a line on the page. "Right here." *Please God, please have her not want to sign this form so I can tell her she can't stay and has to leave.* The sound of Nedra clicking pictures of them doubled in speed.

Marge held her breath, hopeful, but her shoulders slumped when Heloise finally said, "You'll have to be clearer about where you want me to sign this thing."

Marge grudgingly pushed the folder of handouts and their wonderful, thoughtful swag bag in the direction of this miserable person. She barely looked at her guest when pointing toward the elevator and stairway.

"One more thing," Heloise said. "Before I get in too deep with you people, I want to verify that this is indeed a free week's stay. I do not intend to pay for anything while I'm here...especially high-priced meals."

"Yes, it *is* a free week's stay and it most definitely comes with meals. You only pay for personal items that you might buy from the Ship's Store, such as fabric, notions, lip balm, etcetera."

"Why would I want to do that? I'm sure the prices are jacked up so high that everything in your little store is a rip-off."

Marge didn't answer, but took a cleansing breath hoping her blood pressure hadn't gone off the charts. Heloise-with-an-H headed for the elevator.

Returning to the reception area, Rosa sat down and scooted her chair under the table as she leaned over to Marge and whispered, "What a bitch. I'd love to see that one walk the plank right out of here."

"How's Shirley? She seems like such a sweet lady."

"She was pretty rattled but mostly embarrassed. I left her in the capable hands of Sunnie, with some fresh cookies and tea, compliments of Evelyn. They were settling in to have a calming little chat."

"Let's give Beth and Nancy a heads-up in the Quilting Room to keep her as far away from Heloise as possible. We should both make a point to check on Shirley throughout the week."

Phree sent in the next two guests to arrive. They were noisy and loud, in a good / fun type of way, enthusiastic, excited, and thankful to have been chosen for the soft opening. They even squealed when Marge presented them with their official MQR swag bags.

"O.M.G! I already love this place and I'm barely inside the door! This is sooo cool! Thank you, thank you!"

The two happy squealers were followed by a steady stream of quilters all blissfully pleased for a week away from everyday life. Upon entering the building most of the women tilted their heads way back to view the incredible domed ceiling with its gold leaf accents. Without fail the guests expressed their delight: "Wow. Beautiful. I can't wait to see the rest of the building."

By two fifteen in the afternoon the last passenger had been checked in and the Mayflower Quilters Retreat was alive with its new purpose. Several sewing machines were already set up and whirring at the whim of their owners. Women introduced themselves and chatted with fellow quilters over needle, thread, and steaming irons. As Rick rolled the final guest's paraphernalia toward the Hannah Brewster Quilting Room, Marge wondered how the heck he had managed to keep up with the influx of guests and their possessions.

"Rosa, you should be proud of your boy. He did a great job today. I think he's going to be a superstar among the quilting crowd."

"How about it? What a difference a year can make, huh?" The delighted momma smiled. "And for the record…I *am* very, very proud of that boy."

Chapter 5
Beth

Holy Cow! Everything happened at once. One minute Beth was sitting in the quiet Brewster Quilting Room chatting with Nancy about quilts and family and life in general when the first guest arrived.

As much as they fussed over Heloise, it seemed that there was no pleasing her. She didn't want to be too close to the windows, she didn't want to feel penned in or have to 'crawl' over other quilters to get to her machine, and finally, "The smell of coffee nauseates me so don't even *think* about sticking me near that snack area where everyone will be congregating with sticky fingers and cups of hot sloshing liquid."

It didn't take a genius to figure out that this was the person Rosa had warned them about.

Lettie tried to soothe the situation. "Since you're the first quilter here, you have the option to choose wherever you'd like to sit. Pick a station that will work for you and if you need help getting set up…" Lettie paused a beat and with a fake smile added, "Beth over there will be happy to assist you."

From across the room and behind Heloise's back, Beth gave her friend a very unladylike gesture.

Shortly after Heloise had found an acceptable spot, Ricky started making trip after trip with the handcart full of quilting supplies. He piled them along the south wall where the women could easily locate their belongings and then set up their individual stations. Many guests attempted to hand him a tip, but each time Ricky put his hands in the air and shook his head 'no.' There was an MQR rule: The employees of the Pampered Pilgrim Salon & Spa were the only people allowed to accept tips during the week. Tip jars would be placed outside the GM's office for various workers and departments: Housekeeping, Kitchen & Dining, Maintenance, and the only person with their very own jar, Rick Mitchell. Beth felt sure that Ricky's tip jar would be stuffed full by the time the week was over. The women were already joking and teasing with him, and he was playing his part to perfection.

Sunnie had the enviable job of sewing with the passengers for the whole week in the Brewster Quilting Room. She could get a sense of how the retreat flowed, what was working and what was not, and in general act as the eyes and ears of the MQR. There were two small sitting areas for handwork with comfortable chairs and sofas. The plan was that Phree would occasionally stop by to admire the quilters' projects and then settle in to chat and do some handwork with them.

So far, so good—well, that is, with the exception of Heloise.

Beth helped the last two quilters get settled into their stations. They were friends with each other, had arrived in the same car, and wanted to sit together in the quilting room. Unfortunately, the only two stations that were left were far apart from each other. Fortunately, the room was large enough that Nancy and Beth quickly noodled out a plan to have the friends be able to sit side by side.

Chef Evelyn entered the Brewster Quilting Room carrying two trays mounded with mini-croissant sandwiches. She wore a friendly smile on her face and a white chef's jacket with 'MQR Head Chef' emblazoned on the left-hand side. Two kitchen helpers followed behind. One lofted bowls of pasta salad and potato salad, while the other transported a plate of desserts in each hand. Since no lunch was served today due to the timing of check-in, this offering was meant to quell the appetite until dinner could be served at six thirty.

Beth walked the Brewster Quilting Room one final time, making sure everything was in order. The salon tour started in half an hour, and she figured that couldn't possibly take more than fifteen to twenty minutes tops. It had been a long but exhilarating day. With a little luck, she could be in her car by five o'clock and heading home.

Her estimate was close.

It was 5:20 when Beth walked out the door of the MQR accompanied by Helen.

"I'm exhausted," Helen said. "I wonder if we'll ever get used to the craziness of check-in day."

"I'm sure it'll get easier each time. None of us had a clue what to expect today." Beth scratched around in the bottom of her purse, feeling for car keys. "I've got to say, I'm a little envious of all those quilters. There's nothing better than the first day of a quilt retreat. But right now all I want to do is go home and put my feet up. If it wasn't so late I'd even consider taking a nap."

"Late, shmate. That's exactly what I'm going to do," Helen said. "I already texted Ben and told him to figure out something to order for dinner, 'cause I'm gonna do a little toes up first thing when I get home." Helen reached her car before Beth, and the friends said good-bye to each other.

"Till next time," Beth called over her shoulder. Helen was driving down the lane by the time it took Beth to get her key into the ignition.

Reliving the successful and fun feelings of an exciting day, Beth relaxed her head back onto the headrest. It felt good to enjoy the moment and it especially felt good to forget what troubled her. *If I could only...*but only what? *Fill in the blank, Beth, go ahead – If I could only...If I could only stop! If I could only throw things away! If I could only be like everyone else!* How many times had she wished and prayed for this? How many times had she tried?

She put the car in gear and drove out of the MQR parking lot. She had one more errand before she went home and as much as she tried to talk herself out of it, she knew she was going to make that stop.

"I'd like to inquire about prices, please," she told the man behind the counter. A fan oscillated and caught her with a humid breeze every time it methodically swiveled in her direction. Papers and brochures on the desk were moored in place by various items such as a stapler, an unopened water bottle, an empty but smudgy ashtray, and several rather ugly gray rocks.

"Any idea how big you want it, honey?"

The jerk actually winked at her when he said that.

Beth ignored the crude innuendo and tried to sound chipper. "I'm just on a fact-finding mission today. My husband and I don't have a clue how much these things cost." There. It only took her two sentences to mention her husband to this knucklehead...even though telling Tim what she was doing was NOT on the agenda.

"Ah, I see," wheezed the shady-looking proprietor as he retrieved several papers from beneath the low-tech paperweights. "This should tell you everything you need to know."

"How long are the rental periods?"

He reached out a leathery tattooed arm, and with a boney, crooked finger tapped a page on one of the flyers. "Right here. This one has all the details about the time frames and costs. Show this to your hubby, little lady, and he can help you figure it out."

Again the wink.

Little lady? Ugh...chauvinistic, lascivious prick.

Gathering up the papers, Beth left the office of the Whitney Load 'n' Stow Storage Facility feeling insulted and guiltier than ever.

Chapter 6
Marge

"I'd like to get a picture of the four of you standing in that incredible foyer," the photographer from the *Chicago Tribune* said. "And then one in the Brewster Quilting Room with all the quilters as a backdrop. And I think that should do it."

Phree, Marge, Nedra, and Sunnie had replayed this scene on and off all day for various journalists and photographers. They fell into place next to each other, arms around backs, and smiling for the camera. Marge felt a poke, or was it a light pinch on her side just as the camera clicked. From the position of the women on either side of her, Marge figured it had to be Sunnie trying to make her have a wonky smile in the picture. The camera clicked several more times and without moving her lips or losing her practiced grin, Marge pinched back saying, "I can feel that, Sunnie."

On their way to the Quilting Room Marge asked Nedra, "How many more of these do we have scheduled for today?"

"Phree has a short interview with WGN TV. Their producer and video team will also be shooting footage for a special that will air on tonight's news show."

"And then tomorrow we start the process all over again," Phree said.

"Well, the good news is by the time our paying guests arrive at the retreat, all of these distractions will be behind us," Nedra told the group.

This time the photographer wanted to shoot photos of the MQR staff interacting with the quilters. The four women spread out across the room visiting with and getting to know their guests better. Sunnie insisted on a photo of Shirley with a stunning One Block Wonder quilt top which she had added borders to in the few hours she had been here today.

Marge sneaked a look at Heloise while Shirley was being photographed. She could have sworn that steam was escaping through the ears of the ill-tempered woman. Spending time in the Quilting Room with so many creative people was an inspiration, and Marge slipped her cell phone from the pocket of her jeans several times to record images of patterns and fabrics that appealed to her. There were even a few intriguing gadgets that she had never seen before. Not for the first time Marge thought, *This is going to be such a fun job.*

A cluster of women were gathered around one guest enjoying a spontaneous tutorial for a new cutting technique, while at the comfy corner over by the fireplace another group of wool lovers had found each other and were busily sharing stories as they hand stitched intricate pieces with colorful threads. The room seemed to blossom with a positive atmosphere as new friendships were being formed over needle, thread, and fabric.

Zigzagging through the room, Marge stopped to talk or comment on projects with most of the women. *It's good for the retreat if I spend time in here and get input and feedback from our guests.* It was also a fabulous idea to have Sunnie spend the week in the Brewster Room. Right now Sunnie had a captive audience as she told a story of some kind or other while she sat behind her sewing machine ripping out a long seam.

I have to be the luckiest person in the world to be a part of this retreat. I can't imagine anything more satisfying or fun that I could be doing right now. Marge stood at the double pocket doors that were opened to the hallway and as though she were examining a work of art, studied the room from this new angle. When her eye discovered something disturbing she kept her focus on it until she was sure of what she saw. Sitting alone in the midst of storytelling, sharing, and new friendships was Heloise-with-an-H. Back straight and nose to the grindstone, she looked every bit as miserable as Marge suspected her to be.

Heloise didn't look up when Marge approached her station. As a matter of fact, she didn't say a word or in any way even acknowledge that someone was more or less hovering over her. Marge snagged a chair from a nearby station and prayed that the absent woman stayed occupied elsewhere for a little while longer. Sitting in the chair there was still no acknowledgement from Heloise, not even the slightest eye contact.

"What are you working on?" Marge paused for a beat. "It looks beautiful."

Stopping just long enough to send a scathing look over the top of her glasses at the unwelcome intruder, Heloise said, "I'm not much for small talk."

"Okay, I can see that..."

H scoffed.

Marge continued chatting, or trying to chat, as she pretended that she did *not* want to stand up and walk away from this wretched person. "As the general manager I'm hoping to gain some insight from you and all the other guests about your reactions to the retreat so far." Plastering a practiced smile on her face and leaning back in the chair, Marge said, "I know you've only been here a few hours but what are your thoughts up to this point?"

"My first reaction and my biggest complaint..."

Here it comes. Marge braced herself. Everyone involved in the birth of this retreat from Phree, the eight Bunco friends, the construction crew, and the numerous employees had all poured every bit of creativity, love, and elbow grease they could spare to make the MQR a top-notch quilters haven. Now this...this... cantankerous, heartless, poor excuse of a...Marge dialed her disgust down a bit.

"...is the skill level, or should I say, lack of proficiency of the quilters that surround me. I thought this was supposed to be a world-class quilting retreat and instead I find myself among a room full of," Heloise sniffed out the rest of the sentence, "giggling amateurs yakking at each other like a room full of jaybirds."

Marge steepled her fingers over her lips to stifle a nasty comment that threatened to spew forth. So many thoughts ran through her mind that she couldn't get one of them formed into an articulate sentence. She had expected grumbling criticism from this woman about the retreat, but not about the guests...*her* guests.

"In keeping with the spirit of the women and men who came to this country on the Mayflower, we at the Mayflower Quilters Retreat encourage and celebrate all levels of quilt-ability from our guests. That means from beginner to master. From what I've seen so far," Marge paused a beat to get her point across, "we have neither beginner *nor* master in our presence today." Marge reloaded as she stood. "Remember this, Heloise, we will not tolerate quilting police or snobbery at the MQR." Before the stunned know-it-all could speak, Marge turned her back and walked away.

The Bridge, a takeoff on the nautical name given to a ship's control center, was in sight. Her office and harbor from Hurricane Heloise was just a few more steps. Marge would sit behind her desk and regroup. *Have I just been rude to a guest on the very first day? What kind of General Manager am I? Was this a huge mistake to think I could do this job?*

Sunnie, Marge, and Phree each had their own desks in the Bridge. The workspace in the corner was designated for any of the other board members to use as needed. Right now Nedra sat in one of several office chairs at the long table, tapping on the keyboard of a computer.

"Hey Marge. I'll be finished in a few minutes. Just wanna get this new blog post out along with another tweet on

Twitter and a cool photo of the Brewster Room in full swing for Facebook."

Marge was happy for a friendly warm body in the room, but especially pleased for the few moments of silence while her friend updated the MQR social media sites. With elbows on the desk and fingertips resting against her forehead, Marge wondered again if her career move had been a mistake. She hadn't been unhappy being a nurse. She simply thought being the General Manager of the MQR was a once-in-a-late-life opportunity, a chance to do something at which she thought she'd be good and also to be around something she loved: quilting and quilters. *Did I misjudged this situation so terribly?*

A tender touch to her shoulder jolted her to attention.

"You okay, girl?" Nedra said. "What's going on?"

Marge sighed out her friend's name, "Oh, Nedra." She swatted the air in front of her face. "I'm afraid I have no idea what the hell I'm doing."

"That's so un-Marge-like." Nedra rolled Sunnie's office chair over so she could sit across the desk from her troubled friend. "Tell me what's happening."

Marge blurted out something she hadn't realized was bothering her. "Why didn't you take that leave of absence from *Excel* this fall to start your book?"

Nedra registered a genuine look of surprise as she tapped her fingers to her chest. "This is about *me*? You're upset about *me*?"

"No, not exactly," Marge laughed. "I guess I should start at the beginning rather than the middle."

The voices of Sunnie and Phree intruded into the launch of Marge's story as mother and daughter entered the Bridge. "Next up, our first official dinner in the beautiful dining room," Phree said. Taking one look at Marge and Nedra, she added, "What's going on? Is everything okay?"

Seeing mother and daughter together and happy in each other's company gave Marge pause. For the first time in hours, she thought of her sister's e-mail tucked away in her back pocket. But right now she had too many other crazy worries going through her head to open up that can of worms.

"I'm having a moment," Marge said. "I think I might have been somewhat rude to Heloise and now I'm questioning everything."

It was a short rant as Marge explained what had transpired in the Brewster Quilting Room and how it had affected her.

"We have a retreat full of wonderful, fun-loving quilters. Don't let one unhappy soul have that much power over you," Sunnie said.

"It's been a long day and you've done a remarkable job," Phree added. "Many of the women told me how much they love it here and hope to come back someday soon."

"But I want to know," Nedra said, "what does this have to do with my hiatus from *Excel*?"

"I suppose in that very weak moment I thought perhaps I had made a reckless decision when I quit my career to pursue my dream job. I then began to wonder why you had reneged on your plans to take time off to write." Marge pushed a lungful of air past puffed cheeks. "Like Sunnie said, I guess I let one unhappy person get to me."

"Don't go kicking yourself too much," Sunnie said. "Maybe you hit home on a few points and Heloise will actually think about how she's treating people. Besides, we all question ourselves at times. That's what keeps us honest so we don't turn into the next version of Heloise…or Laura."

"Good point," Phree said.

Marge looked at Nedra. *She is always so put together.* Even though they were all wearing the same MQR polo shirts, her friend's dark skin was complimented by the pink rather than washed out like her own pale coloring and gray head of hair. "So what gives, Lange. What happened to the six-month writer's break you were going to take this fall after your girls went back to college?"

"Well, a couple of things. The most important reason why I haven't done it yet is because I didn't feel it was smart to take time away from work to write a novel only to be swamped with getting the social media sites up and running for the retreat. I knew the amount of work was going to be labor intensive to get the MQR set up the way I wanted it. In a few more months, maybe even weeks, we'll be organized enough that all of us will be tweeting and adding our own Facebook and blog updates."

"I guess that makes sense," Marge said. "Do you ever question if you should do it?"

"Yes but no." Nedra laughed. "Sure there are moments when I'm afraid, but I know in my heart it's the right thing for me to do at this time in my life. To tell the truth Marge, I was inspired by what you did. I'm not sure if I would have attempted such a wacky idea had you not quit your nursing job to work here."

"Thanks for the vote of confidence, Nedra, but I certainly second-guessed myself up one side and down the other for a few minutes today." Glancing at the wall clock Marge added, "Looks like it's time that we head over to the dining room. I'd like the four of us to greet the guests and help them get settled at their tables for the first time. I'm sure there'll be questions about the procedures to follow for dining."

"I was thinking that us four might spread out and share the meal with some of the quilters tonight," Sunnie said. "What do you think about that, oh wise GM?"

"I think that's a great idea, Sunnie but please don't stick me with Heloise. I think I've done enough damage today where she's concerned."

"It might be time that I met up with this woman," Sunnie said. "I think I'll do her the dubious honor of joining her for dinner tonight."

Marge felt relieved and said to Phree, "Did I ever

mention that your mother is a saint?"

Chapter 7
Beth

Sunday evening at the Stevenson home was usually subdued as the members of the family each prepared for the next morning and the beginning of their work or school week. Unless there was some sort of emergency, Beth would not go back to the retreat until Wednesday, the day that she was slated to work at the Pampered Pilgrim Salon. She already had two haircuts and styles on the books along with a no-chip manicure, two pedicures, and an eyebrow waxing. It seemed as though many of the quilters liked the idea of a little time off from projects to pamper themselves.

Beth hadn't yet closed the kitchen door behind her when one of the twins ran toward her. "Mom, Mom, you'll never guess what Dad said!" Thirteen-year-old Katy slammed into her mother as she encircled her in a hug.

"Whoa, slow down, honey." Sharing the embrace and enjoying the nearness of a child, Beth smoothed her daughter's hair. "What's all the excitement about?"

"Dad said that Joey and I could have a Ping-Pong table like the Swansons do if you say it's okay. He said you'd have to agree because it would go down in the basement with all your junk." Katy took several small hops on her tippy-toes while shaking her fisted hands by her chest. "Can we? Can we? Pleeeeease say it's okay!" More hopping with cheerleader pulsing fists.

"What do you mean, with all my junk?"

Katy stopped hopping and stared at her mother. "Huh?"

"You said because the Ping-Pong table would go down in the basement with all of my junk. What do you mean by that?" Beth was feeling cornered and sounding defensive. By the confused look on her daughter's face, she needed to slow down a bit. "I mean there's not that much stuff down there anymore. We got rid of most of it in February."

"No, not that junk."

Beth sensed her daughter's confusion lessen.

"It's because your salon and sewing studio are down there. He said there's plenty of room for a Ping-Pong table and some chairs and other cool stuff, but that we might be too noisy and disturb you. Especially when you're working in the salon."

It was true that the family more or less considered the basement to be her domain.

Joey slid into the uncarpeted room on his stockinged feet, like Tom Cruise had done in the movie, *Risky Business.* "Whadshe say?" He stumbled the last few yards and windmilled into Katy.

The twins laughed and Katy said, "Get off me! You're such a nerd!"

Beth made her way past the siblings as they playfully swatted at each other. "Is Heather home? Where's your father?"

"Heather's in her room studying as usual and Dad's down in the basement measuring things," Joey said. "Ouch! Make her stop hitting me, Mom."

Beth felt herself grow pale at the thought of Tim rambling around the basement at will. She could hear the blood pulse in her ears and felt heat with an immediate tightening growing in her chest. *I should have gotten that stuff out of there a long time ago.* Beth knew her mild-mannered hubby would feel betrayed by her deceit, and her mind scrambled in case she had to offer him an acceptable explanation. *How long has he been down there? What is he doing?*

Has he discovered that all of my stuff is still down there and that I've lied to him? Beth held her breath and tuned out the twins, needing to see the look on her husband's face when he walked into the kitchen.

Joey came over to her and slung an arm around her shoulder. "Hey, best Mom in the world." He was only a drop shorter than she was. Beth figured that somewhere around Christmastime this year she would start spending the rest of her life looking up to see into her little boy's face. "Now that we can have friends over since all the junk is out of this place, it would be so cool to have Ping-Pong tournaments and parties like the Swansons do." He crushed her in a hug, and in a fake little-boy voice added, "I wuv you, Mommy."

Beth had to laugh and she even relaxed a little. "I love you too, you little schemer."

Tim called out as he walked upstairs from the basement, "Give your mother a chance to unwind before you pummel her with any more questions."

That sounds promising, doesn't it?

Rounding the corner from the hall where the basement stairs were, Tim looked at a tablet, tapping it with the eraser end of a pencil. "I think there's plenty of room to make the Stevensons' Ping-Pong Palace a reality," he said.

The twins shrieked and hooted. Joey punched the air above his head with his fist and Katy continued her hopping-clapping-cheering routine.

"Hang on, you two. Give Mom some time to hear the plans and think this through." Tim bent over and gave his wife a tender kiss on the cheek. Under his breath he said, "Sorry they nailed you as you walked in the door."

Beth took her first full breath since she found out her hubby was in the basement. *He mustn't know. How can he not see what's going on down there?* Her mind flashed to the many times she wore a new blouse, had her hair styled by someone other than herself, or an item or scent that made her feel especially attractive, and the fact that Tim rarely noticed. She had long since gotten over the hurt feelings she first felt by his lack of awareness—it just wasn't who he was. Tim Stevenson was a history professor and enthusiast, a bookworm, and a scholar. He was *not* a visual person and right about now, Beth was pretty happy with his personality traits. The exception was that he occasionally threw her a curveball and noticed something obscure; she never knew when it was coming.

This is still a very dangerous situation.

"I think it will be good for the twins. You know…keep 'em off the streets and stuff." At the kitchen table over their standard Sunday-night fare of pizza dinner, the Stevensons' firstborn shared her opinions about the possibility of a Ping-Pong table with her parents.

Beth reached for one more pizza slice and chose a large portion. *This is the final piece. No more.* "It's not exactly like they're on the streets, Heather," she said.

"Okay then, keep 'em off the video game kick that they seem determined to make into their life's occupation." Heather was in her first semester of Culinary Arts at Joliet Junior College. Her joy at recently finding the path she was meant to follow had caused her to be somewhat judgmental toward others—especially her siblings.

"Honey, I'm thrilled that you love what you're doing, but I seem to remember someone who was floundering until she accepted the gastronomic talent that was brewing under all those video games that *you* played for years."

"Whatever." Heather rolled her eyes toward the ceiling and shook her head at the same time. "I still think the Ping-Pong thing is a good idea, but be prepared to have a bunch of hormonal idiotic teens hanging out here."

"That's just the point," Tim said. "They'll be here and so will Mom most of the time. Even if she's in the salon or sewing studio, it will be hard for the kids to pull something over on your mother."

Heather held her palms up shoulder high. "You're not telling me anything I don't already know. Mom has some kind of extrasensory hearing or sight or something. I could never get away with anything."

"It's called being a mother," Beth laughed. "It comes with that final push through the birth canal."

"Eewww," Heather said. "I'm trying to eat here."

Joey and Katy sat on the floor in the family room, backs against the sofa, taking quick bites of pizza while competing for a win on their favorite video game.

Beth knew she was trapped. She had to approve this scheme or come across as the bad guy. She wished Tim would had tossed this idea out to her first so they could have discussed the pros and cons, but learned that after spending several hours at the Swansons' playing Ping-Pong with a group of friends, the twins had come home begging their father for the latest cool thing to have.

"It always pays to be the meeting place for teens," Tim said. "That way you know where your kids are." Tim stood over the pizza, removing the leftovers from the box onto a paper plate. "The tricky part is for one of the parents to be there at the same time. With Mom running her business out of the home, we're able to do that. It's a luxury that a lot of people don't have."

Heather leaned back in her chair and stretched her arms over her head. "I admit it was always nice to have Mom here when I got home from school."

She didn't know it, but Heather had just cinched the deal for her brother and sister.

It's important that I make this work somehow, Beth thought. I'll figure out something to do with my collection.

Chapter 8
Marge

The dining room, or Quilters Mess Hall, was comfortably large and had been artfully planned to account for various dining personalities. Seating ranged from a few two-tops that provided an atmosphere for intimate conversations, to the middle of the room with a number of square expandable four-tops along with three round tables that seated six, and finally a gently curving banquette running the length of the longest wall. In constructing this beautiful dining area additional space had been 'borrowed' from a nonessential hallway. The increased size liberated the room from a confined dark space where fifty-plus nuns sat side by side on benches at long tables as they ate meals three times a day, into the luxurious fine-dining room suitable for a group of hungry, motivated quilters.

Marge was pleased at the passengers' reactions when the doors to the Mess Hall were finally opened and they viewed the room for the first time. She noted how the quilters, all keen observers, stopped to point out details to each other. Cameras and cell phones were raised and pointed at the salon-sized painting hanging over the banquette section. Phree had commissioned a local artist to paint a magnificent portrait of the Mayflower in roiling waters nearing the North American shore. It truly was a breathtaking room that transported happy thread-laden quilters from the productive and busy Brewster Room to an elegant dining experience.

Sunnie moved close to Marge and whispered, "Isn't it fun to think that this unveiling will be played over and over with a different group of quilters every Sunday evening at the

MQR?"

"I don't think I'll ever grow tired of witnessing this scene," answered Marge.

A woman pointed her camera at the two of them and said, "Can I get a few shots of you for my quilting blog?" Her camera flashed, and then she said, "Could you stand under the painting?"

Others agreed and readied their devices as Sunnie called out to Phree and Nedra to join them. "Might as well get all of us in the photo," she said.

The four women were dwarfed under the enormous piece of artwork as they snugged together and posed with arms around each other's backs. Every woman with a camera or phone rushed to click an image of the MQR staff. Marge heard comments of "Perfect," "I love it," and "I don't have a camera with me—would you e-mail me a copy?"

When the photo frenzy had died down, Marge called out, "Ladies, let's find our seats. We don't want our dinner getting cold." Marge had kept an eye on Heloise during the uproar from the introduction of the dining room. Of course, she had not participated in the enthusiasm. Instead she had sat at a table for two, her back to the crowd, nibbling warm slices of bread.

Mouthing 'Good luck' to Sunnie, Marge watched her weave through the diners toward Heloise. *Talk about the sacrificial lamb.*

Sunnie Easton had been a hippie for all of her adult life. You only had to take a look at her to know that she marched to a different tune. A little over a year ago when her daughter and only child, Phreedom Aquarius, known as Phree, was finally able to realize her longtime dream of owning a quilters retreat, there were several personal issues that Sunnie and her daughter successfully conquered in order to move forward with their relationship. With Sunnie's background in community service and counseling, she was a valuable addition to the Mayflower Quilters Retreat as the assistant general manager.

Phree and Nedra each found a table of quilters with at least one empty chair, and the diners appeared to enthusiastically include them each as a member of their dinner group. As Marge passed tables of diners, she stopped to chat for a moment before moving on to the next..."Everything okay here ladies?" ... "Do you need anything?" ... "How's it going with the hexie group?"

The waitstaff, including Ricky Mitchell, began to carry out and serve the family style dinner. Breakfast and lunch would be served buffet style during a preset span of time, but dinner would be served as a restaurant-style meal every evening at six thirty. Marge located an open chair at the table where Shirley was seated.

"May I join you ladies for dinner?"

"Oh, by all means. We'd love to have your company."

Camaraderie was off the charts in the dining room and Marge relished every minute of it. "Are you ladies enjoying your stay so far?"

"We've only been here about four hours and already the MQR has exceeded my expectations."

"This isn't just a retreat," one woman said as she picked several wayward threads from her sweater. "It's an experience."

Did anyone have suggestions for improvements? ...Absolutely none.

"I'm especially enjoying all of the Mayflower and ship references," Patrice said as she lifted the cloche off a platter of meats and took a second helping. "I also love how there are corresponding plaques explaining the connections to the ship and the Pilgrims. I've already learned so many new facts."

Ricky scurried from table to table with two carafes of coffee, and Marge watched as the guests laughed and kibitzed with him. More than once she heard someone call in a singsong voice, "Oh, Rick, could I have a refill over here?"

Marge felt motherly pride toward Rosa's son, who was working hard to overcome the ugly ordeal from a year ago that had nearly ruined his young life.

Steering the conversation first toward personal discussions and then finally the one thing they all had in common—quilting—Marge wondered how only an hour ago she could have doubted her decision to be the general manager of this wonderful retreat. When the dessert carts began to roll through the dining room, Marge excused herself and wandered between the tables conversing with the guests who chose to linger over their sweets. No she was not on a diet and, yes, she loved dessert as much as everyone...but she also knew that at some point during the evening meal, Chef Evelyn had instructed a server to deliver a tray of sweets to the GM's office, where Marge would savor the treats and celebrate a successful day with a hot cup of tea and three dear friends before heading home tonight.

"If you have any energy left, tell me everything," Marge's husband, Bud, said as he pulled a cork out of a bottle of wine. "I've been waiting all day to hear the details."

Marge lounged on the sofa, and the simple pleasure of sinking into her favorite slippers almost made her weep with joy. "I'm sure I'm past exhaustion, but unfortunately my adrenaline is still pumping at breakneck speed."

Handing his wife a wineglass, Bud said, "I think this might help you unwind."

"My hero." Marge sighed and proceeded to recount the high points of the day to her husband. It took two more glasses of wine and a little over an hour for her to get through the stories from the maiden voyage of the MQR.

"What did she find out?" Bud asked after he heard that Sunnie volunteered to eat with the dreaded Heloise, or H as they now called the cantankerous woman for short.

"Not much, really. H remained pretty tight-lipped even

with Sunnie. She's your typical know-it-all bossy pants with a horrible attitude." Marge drained the last few drops from her glass and let out a long breath. "The four of us concluded that when you get a large enough group of people together for whatever reason, there always seems to be a know-it-all in the bunch. We'd better get used to the idea that to some degree or other we'll most likely have a new one or two joining us every week at the retreat."

Marge was fighting to keep her eyes open, and when she finally let go with a yawn the size of an overtired lion, Bud reached over and slipped the wineglass from his wife's hand, saying, "Looks like the wine might have finally caught up to your adrenaline, babe."

Opting to sleep an extra half hour in the morning and skip breakfast at home, Marge planned to snag a bowl of oatmeal and a banana from the Quilter's Mess Hall when she arrived at work. There was no longer any need to check e-mails at home in the morning. She had asked Nedra yesterday to set up her two personal accounts so she would be able to access her communications privately at the retreat. Sure, she could use her phone for that, but they were attempting to maintain a policy with the staff of no cell phone usage while working. Marge hoped to set a good example, but after receiving Laura's e-mail yesterday, she became aware of the need to stay in contact with her family while at work.

Slipping the Monday morning MQR polo shirt, forest green with white embroidery, over her head after a shower, Marge blew her hair dry, and then transferred the folded letter into the back pocket of today's clean jeans. Marge was ready for another day, and that surely would bring new experiences as well as new challenges. She tugged a warm sweater from one of many pegs by the back door of the Russell home and headed into the crisp coolness of a drizzly September morning.

Last night music from the radio had helped her stay

alert during the fifteen-minute drive from the MQR, but this morning she switched off the volume. These fifteen minutes might be the only time today she would be able to ponder the scathing e-mail her sister had sent. When her cell phone rang only a half block from home, Marge pushed the button on her Bluetooth earpiece to be in compliance with Illinois's 'hands free' cell phone law.

"Hello?"

"Hi, Mom." It was her daughter. The sound of Val's voice sent Marge's mommy radar off the charts. The mere way those two words were spoken told Marge that there was a serious problem. Val was in her first semester at Northern Illinois University only ninety minutes away.

"You okay?" Marge asked. "You sound upset."

"Yeah. I...I guess I'm okay. I mean there's nothing *really* wrong."

Marge gripped the wheel a little tighter and toyed with pulling over somewhere so she could give Val her full attention. "What do you mean by, 'there's nothing *really* wrong'?" Fearing the worst scenarios that she could conjure, Marge visualized her daughter bruised, bleeding or, God forbid, abused in some way.

"It's just that...well, I feel like such a baby."

Marge could tell that her daughter desperately tried to sound as though she was not crying—actually it was more like sobbing. Marge pulled onto a side street and stopped the car. Her hammering heart was nearly about to crash through her chest while fear embraced her with a crushing grip. Her world had collapsed into a tiny bubble of panic around her and all that existed was her daughter's troubled voice. "Take a deep breath, honey and tell me what's going on."

A sob boiled from the phone and Marge instantly thought, *I can be there in 90 minutes. Sunnie can take over for me at the retreat.*

"I'm just...I miss you and Dad so much. I want to come

home. I don't want to be away." Val coughed out a sad, weeping sound. "I tried to stick it out, but I'm miserable. I want to quit school and come home."

So many feelings washed over Marge at once that she felt like an emotional chameleon—relief, sadness, confusion, worry, and even a pinch of anger were the main feelings troubling her soul. "How long has this been going on?"

"From the beginning...when you and Dad drove away after you dropped me off that first day."

"Has someone been mean to you or hurt you in some way?" Marge wanted to find out if Val's story was just a ruse and deeper concerns lay beneath.

"No. Everyone is great. That's part of the problem I think. I feel like a freak. I mean everyone is so happy to be away from home and all I want to do is go back home and be with my family."

"Honey, it's been six weeks. You must be over the worst part by now. Can't you just..."

"No! I hate it!" And then, "I'm lonely." She was crying in earnest now, long sobs that sounded hopeless. "I'm a failure. I'm a baby. I hate myself."

Marge heard a dull thud. "What was that noise? Did you hit something?"

"No. I cut the corner too sharp and ran into the doorframe."

Marge wasn't sure she believed the excuse. She had not expected this from Val—Val the girl who was everyone's friend, Val who had no fear about new adventures, Val who had waited impatiently the past two years to go away to college. Thinking fast, Marge said, "I have all of Wednesday and Thursday off work." Marge had planned and looked forward to spending some sewing time with the guests by going to the retreat for part of those days. "Can you wait until either of those days? I'll come out to Dekalb and we can have lunch and maybe do a little shopping or get manicures. How does that sound?"

"Oh, Mom! I'd love that. Wednesday...let's do it Wednesday. That means I only have to wait today and tomorrow and you'll be here the next day."

More broken sobs came over the phone, but Marge could imagine the smile spread across her daughter's blotchy red face through her enthusiastic reply.

"My last class on Wednesday is over at one o'clock." Sniffles were rampant. "We could spend the day together. I just...I just can't wait to see you."

"Let's do it!" Marge said a little too eagerly as she tapped her directional signal and pulled back onto the road. She thought to herself that she could spend a few hours in the morning at the MQR, leave about eleven o'clock, and make it to NIU easily by one o'clock. "Hang in there, sweetie. We'll have a nice afternoon together and you can tell me about what's going on."

"I've gotta go, Mom. My class started a few minutes ago....I love you."

"I love you too, Val." Marge was encouraged that her daughter was still concerned about getting to class on time. *That has to be a good sign...right?* She had two days to learn everything she could about college kids being homesick.

But Marge's finely tuned radar told her something more was 'off' with her daughter. She couldn't quite put her finger on it aside from the fact that this overall behavior was so *not* Val. Could she have gotten involved with drugs or alcohol or some unsavory boy? Or is she simply struggling with her classes?

Pulling into the Mayflower Quilters Retreat employee parking lot, Marge thought, *Now I have two things that I need to discuss with Sunnie.*

Chapter 9
Val

Val tapped her cell phone off and fingered the spot on the back of her skull where, out of anger and frustration, she had smacked her head on the wall while she was talking to her mom. She knew she deserved the pain for being such a stupid jerk, but what the heck did she think she was going to solve by hurting herself? Why had she told her mother she had to get to class? Why couldn't she just tell her the truth? Surely of all the people in the world, her mom would understand.

Valerie Russell hadn't been to any of her classes for the past week. For the five weeks before, her attendance had been spotty at best. She felt weak, ashamed, lonely, lost, and most of the time physically ill. She didn't know what she could possibly do at this point that wouldn't disappoint her parents. No matter how much she cried, the tears kept coming and her nose was crazy runny all of the time.

All she wanted to do was go home and hide her shame from everyone.

Chapter 10
Beth

Morning didn't feel especially refreshing after Beth had been worried and anxious all night. Somewhere between 3:30 and 4:00 a.m. she finally dozed off into a light sleep. Several times, she had cautiously exited the bed that she shared with her husband, The Deep Sleeper. She often envied his ability to nod off fast and stay asleep all night, but she was never more jealous than last night. Her chest had burned with anxiety, and several times she felt adrenaline kick in so hard that her heart rate soared to the point where her sinuses even tingled. Beth knew an anxiety attack when she had one, and last night's multiple occurrences would go down in her own personal record book as a doozy.

The minute the kids were all off to school and Tim had left for work, Beth was on the move. She slid her keys from the counter, snatched her purse, and checked it for the Whitney Load 'n' Stow application and brochures she had filled out. She tried to stay calm as she did the one thing she had promised herself she'd never do—irreversibly deceive her husband.

A nippy fall rain began halfway to the storage rental. It pounded down like a random drumbeat, and she waited in the car for it to slow to a pace where she could run without her umbrella—which *wasn't* in the car where it was supposed to be. The short drive did nothing to give her a new perspective or calm her breathing in any way. Waiting for the rain to pass gave her an opportunity to study the pamphlet the randy, winking man behind the counter had given her last night.

She was surprised at what she considered to be rather hefty rental charges, but didn't have the time or luxury of shopping around. Besides, if she dragged her feet for too long they might just get cold, and she really needed to move forward. In her opinion there were no other options at this point. Now to decide on the size; her stomach flipped over for what surely *had* to be the hundredth time today.

Beth hadn't noticed the tinkling bell on the door when she was here last night. No one sat on the stool behind the counter, but she could hear a rustling of papers from the back room. She was happy to see that Mr. Winker was not the person who pushed aside the curtain to attend to the customer. Instead, a grandmother-type carrying a McDonald's breakfast sandwich in a hastily wrapped wad of yellow paper asked with a slight twang, "Can I help you, hon?"

Beth wondered if Grandma Twang and Mr. Winker were a couple.

It took a remarkably short time, maybe only forty minutes, and Beth was walking back to her car carrying a set of keys for a small unit with a rental lease of six months. Feeling better than she had since she entered her home last night, she quietly said, "Dang that was easy. Maybe I should have done this a long time ago." She would pack up the car as many times as was needed, get her collection of bins over here, and the twins could soon revel in the joys of the new Stevenson Ping-Pong Palace.

Thank goodness the rain had stopped while she was busy deceiving Tim.

The weight and searing heat that had recently taken up residence in her chest were gone as a smile punctuated her short-lived feeling of confidence.

By the time Beth wrestled the third carload of bins over to the Load 'n' Stow and stacked them into the ever-shrinking storage space, her newfound confidence had been chipped away to reveal the more familiar feelings of guilt and fear. Humidity from the brief shower had coupled with sunshine and heat to turn her into a sweaty mess from the activity of hoisting and hefting the plastic containers. Learning an important trick many years ago, she had been smart enough to only buy the biggest size plastic container that she could handle on her own.

What had she been thinking, for God's sake? How was renting a storage shed behind her family's back a solution? She needed to just throw away this stuff and be done with it. Start over with a clean slate. Stop all this subterfuge and be a normal person…wife…mother. But she knew she couldn't. The anxiety was too great, and if she was being honest, it was getting worse.

With an eye to the clock, Beth decided this would have to be her last trip today. The twins would be home soon, and she still had to shower and get ready for her first client. She had phoned her five appointments this morning and asked if they could reschedule for two hours later because something unexpected needed her attention. Three of the woman could switch, no problem, but two had to cancel and reschedule for later in the week. Around four thirty she would text Tim at the college and explain to him that she had a tight schedule because someone showed up late and could he pick up something for dinner.

More lies.

Hefting the last bin of the day onto a waist-high stack, Beth swabbed at her sticky forehead with the back of her hand as she studied the proof of her deception. Wanting to cry yet afraid she might never stop, she began to second-guess what had seemed like a genius idea only a few short hours ago. *Will the lies never end?*

Probably not.

Beth's at-home one-chair salon was in the basement of

the Stevensons' home and had its own entryway from the outside. Two weekends ago Tim had removed the leggy and spent summer annuals from the decorative pots adorning the small deck outside the salon's entrance. Cheerful and colorful fall mums in yellows and reds now greeted her customers when they arrived. Nothing centered Beth more than the routine of her salon and its established clientele. By the time she had Mrs. Adams' hair washed and was ushering her to the beauty chair, Beth had compartmentalized the morning's activities and slipped them into the 'think about it later' slot in her brain.

"It seems weird to be here on a Monday," Jane Adams said. "For all the years you've been styling my hair, I've always come on Wednesdays." She sputtered a little. "Well, I didn't mean that it's a big deal or anything…just that I'm used to Wednesdays. But I understand and I think it's a great opportunity to start styling hair at the retreat. Are you going to be okay with this new schedule?"

"I'll be fine. When I offered to work the salon at the Mayflower Quilters Retreat, I needed to do something to accommodate my clients who were regulars on Wednesday. I should be thanking you for being flexible enough to switch days." Beth's instinctive use of styling shears combined with her flair for what was trending had earned her a reputation among her steady customers, so much so that about six years ago she had stopped taking new customers.

"Tell me about the retreat. I saw a report on the news last night and it looks like some kind of an expensive mansion or something." Jane spoke a little faster. "Is there any way us nonquilting town people might get inside for a tour?"

"Actually, that's a great idea, Jane. I'll bring it up to Phree." A tour or two would be a show of goodwill with the locals, and from what Beth was hearing, *everyone* in town was curious and talking about the place. She was sure that Phree would like the idea and wondered why none of them had thought about it themselves.

By the time Beth unsnapped and skillfully glided the hair-studded cape away from Jane's body, she could hear some rustling and scraping coming from the basement beyond the salon's wall. It had to be Tim. The twins rarely came downstairs for any reason other than when she asked them to retrieve something for her. While waiting for Jane's charge card to be approved, a fresh wave of anxiety gripped her chest with a tightening fist. She prayed that Jasmine would be late for her appointment so she could take a peek at who was doing what on the other side of the wall.

The door to the basement was in the back room of her salon. Beth cracked it open a tiny bit, just big enough to see Tim standing with his hands on his hips staring at one of the walls where last February she had parked the plastic tubs three deep. She heard blood swishing in her ears and felt her heart pick up its pace to about a million beats per minute. At the sound of the door creaking, Tim spun around and locked eyes with his wife.

"What's up?" Beth tried to sound firm and confident but didn't feel either.

"Just working out the logistics for the upcoming Ping-Pong table acquisition. You?"

"I thought I heard something going on back here and Jasmine's late so I had time to check it out. She usually runs about fifteen minutes behind."

"I've been thinking about something…"

Here it comes!

"What if I soundproof your salon so when the kids are down here you won't have to hear them and neither will your clients. I think it wouldn't be too hard." He walked over to the back side of the longest wall of the salon, patted an exposed two-by-four about shoulder high, and let his hand rest there. "This is the only wall exposed to the part of the basement where the kids will be." He pointed to one end of the salon that butted up against an outside wall. "That end is a nonissue and," pointing to the other end said, "with your sewing studio tied in to the other end, so is that one."

Beth nodded her head, barely able to breathe full breaths in and out. *How could he not notice that there's a big gap in the containers where I removed three carloads of bins today?*

"...and then I'll cover the drywall with cheap carpeting. I think very little noise will get through."

She had missed half of his explanation but her husband looked so proud she just said, "Wow, that's a great idea but it sounds like a lot of work." She weighted a thought for a moment and then added, "Come with me, I want to show you something."

Her husband followed her back inside the salon. She led him to the area where the back-stock of products she sold to her clients was shelved. Next to the shelves hung the only picture in the room; a small framed photo of a sultry smiling model was dangling crookedly. Beth used her best Vanna White impression to point out the lovely frame and said, "I want to keep this."

Tim's brows came together and his eyes went toward the ceiling as Beth watched her hubby trying to figure out the riddle.

"I...uh. Sure. Okay. You can keep it."

Finally Beth said, "It's not the picture I'm talking about." She removed the frame from a hook in the wall. "It's what's behind it."

Tim's eyes went wide and he smiled. "Well aren't you the sneaky one." His wife was shorter than him by a head, and he bent over and put his eye to a hole approximately the size a paper puncher would make. "I can see the whole basement from here."

"Exactly."

"How did I never notice this from the other side?"

Beth smiled and wasn't surprised as she replaced the picture. "Take a look out there." She had hammered a small screwdriver to punch through the drywall. She did it from the basement side into the backroom so surrounding chips were 'knocked-out' into the salon. All you could see from the basement was a small black circle shape. Using a Sharpie pen, she drew several similar sized 'holes' randomly on the drywall so the real one didn't stand out so much. The pouty model in her frame and a strategically placed small piece of duct tape prevented the light from inside the salon's back room from pouring into the inner basement.

"I'm going to have to start calling you James Bond," Tim said. "This is genius. You'll be able to actually see if anything gets hormonally crazy down here and stop it before it goes too far."

"It's a little low-tech but it gets the job done." Beth wasn't about to explain that the actual reason for the hole was to spy on him to make sure he left her collection alone.

"I'd be willing to bet that you've got one of these in your sewing studio too."

Beth smiled at her handsome but clueless husband, "Ya think?"

Chapter 11
Marge

The morning rain coaxed yellow and orange leaves loose from trees surrounding the Mayflower Quilters Retreat. Colorful foliage drifted toward the manicured lawn, slick with rainwater and fragrant with the earthy scent of fall. Even though Marge had been working at the retreat since late June, this was only the second full day that the retreat was operating with guests in attendance. Eager to get inside and take the baton from Sunnie, Marge quickened her pace as she dialed down her mommy radar and her concerns over Val. It was time to wall up her personal life and focus on work.

Three quilters were hand quilting and chatting as they sat in rocking chairs on the massive covered porch. One of the women was piecing intricate Cathedral Window blocks while another was stitching a wool applique Penny Rug. The third guest had a cup of coffee in her hand, a pair of binoculars for birdwatching around her neck, and a small wooden basket of hexies in her lap.

As much as she wanted to remember everyone's name, Marge had never been good at that particular skill, so instead she went with a generic greeting as she walked up the steps. "Good morning, ladies."

There had been some discussion about screening in the porch to keep it free from mosquitoes, bees, and other pesky bugs, but the consensus had been to wait until spring and then decide if that was necessary.

Smiling, the women chorused, "Hi Marge."

The bird-watcher held up her binoculars. "I thought I

might see some fall migrators but as a passenger on the Mayflower, I find myself looking for land instead."

Marge laughed and felt validated that the Mayflower theme was being enjoyed. Reaching the top step she asked, "May I take a peek?" She understood the importance of making the quilters feel welcome as she remembered her own words at the staff pep rally the other day: "We want our guests to feel like they are part of our family at the Mayflower Quilters Retreat."

"I haven't felt this relaxed in years," Cathedral Window said. "This has already been a wonderful experience and we're only beginning our second day."

Binoculars, who had to be at least in her seventies said, "I was just telling Anne and Flo that I want your job when I grow up."

"You'll have to arm wrestle me for it," Marge smiled. "I think it's got to be about the best job in the world for a quilter."

The others agreed with head bobs and an, "Amen to that."

"I had best get to my office before Phree comes out here and offers you my job," Marge joked. "I'll catch you ladies later. Happy stitching."

The moment she opened the door to the retreat the unmistakable scent of maple bacon and fresh brewed coffee filled the foyer, and Marge's mouth began to water. *That's what I get for skipping breakfast.*

Sunnie looked up from her desk as Marge entered the Bridge. "Morning, Marge. Were you able to get any sleep last night?"

"By the time I unwound after telling Bud everything about the day and we shared a bottle of wine, I slept like a baby being rocked on board a ship." She took her cell phone and tube of lip balm out of her purse, slipped them in the pockets of her jeans, and then stowed her purse in the employee closet. "How'd it go here?"

Sunnie leaned back in her office chair and gently swiveled it from side to side. "Well, let's see…Heloise hunted me down and threatened to leave if the group in the corner by the minibar didn't grow up and stop cackling at everything." Putting up her two hands, she made air quotes when she said "cackling" and rolled her eyes at the same time. "That woman is definitely a buzzkill."

"And we still don't know anything about her?"

"Not a thing…well, other than the obvious that she's a pain in the butt. She's as tight as a tick when it comes to giving out information about herself but she sure is free with advice about how everyone else should behave."

"I'm going to head over to the dining room and bring back some breakfast on a tray. Then you can get me up to speed on the details of life with Heloise and anything else I need to know."

"Sounds good." Sunnie licked an envelope and then said, "Wait till you see the spread in there. All I can say is wow! Speaking of which, could you snag me another cinnamon roll—they're incredible."

"You got it."

Marge made the short hike down the corridor to the Quilters Mess Hall. After the phone call from Val this morning, she *had* to make it a priority to talk to Sunnie sometime today. She wanted sound and unbiased input from her experienced friend. Certainly Sunnie would have some insight about how to handle her homesick daughter. The tickle of a mother's sixth sense kicked in again, and Marge couldn't shake the feeling that there was more to Val's story.

Breakfast buffet was served from six thirty till nine o'clock and anything that was not eaten would be placed on a table until eleven for the late risers. Chef Evelyn didn't want any of the guests going without a meal and had insisted that a cold breakfast was better than no breakfast at all. Stainless steel warming trays with domed acrylic roller lids contained a myriad of breakfast items. A stunning Eggs Benedict resting on a generous slice of Canadian bacon with a divine drizzle of hollandaise sauce over the whole creation immediately found its way onto Marge's plate. Surely even Gordon Ramsay would be proud of this culinary achievement. Warm sausage gravy was waiting to top light and fluffy buttermilk biscuits, maple flavored bacon layered the bottom of another warming tray, and a pitcher of clear golden-brown syrup sat next to a warmer filled with blueberry studded pancakes. A crystal bowl showed off fresh cut fruit as bejeweled art, while pastry, muffins, and quick breads were displayed on raised serving stands. Fresh squeezed juice along with coffee and tea rounded out the morning feast.

When the MQR board members had sat down with Chef Evelyn it had been decided, among many other details, that the first breakfast the quilters would experience on Monday morning during their week at the retreat should be an elegant affair. Marge thought the kitchen crew did not disappoint.

Handing Sunnie her plated cinnamon roll, Marge said, "Boy you weren't kidding. Wow doesn't even come close, but I can't think of a better adjective for what the kitchen just pulled off." Placing the breakfast tray on her desk and sitting on the office chair, she rolled toward her food. "Fill me in on anything I need to know."

While Marge worked her way through the plate of food in front of her, Sunnie recapped the highlights of the overnight happenings. There wasn't a lot to tell, and by the time Marge had finished her breakfast, Sunnie said, "So basically other than the little hissy fit from Heloise early on and the late-night group sharing two bottles of wine, I'd say our first night was a nonevent."

"That's good to hear. Let's hope the nights stay that way." Folding her cloth napkin and placing it on top of the empty plate, Marge added, "I'm glad you were able to get a good night's sleep with no interruptions."

"I suspect that's going to be par for the course unless there's some kind of rare emergency around here." Sunnie placed her hands palm down on the desk and pushed to a standing position. "What's on the agenda today?"

"*Outside* this room we are living in the moment, happy to be around our guests, and enjoying their company. *Inside* this room we are getting ready for next week with an eye toward the week after that." Marge pushed her tray aside, opened a manila folder, and took out an Excel spreadsheet. "Nedra will be in today around nine," Marge looked up at Sunnie. "You do know that she took the week off work at *Excel* to handle our computer sites and media appointments?" When Sunnie nodded her head, Marge continued. "Phree will roll in at some point and…"

Sunnie interrupted. "Phree's already here. She poked her head in the door about twenty minutes ago and said she was heading to the Brewster Quilting Room."

"Good. She told me yesterday that she was planning to spend time today visiting and stitching with the passengers."

"This is only the beginning of our second day with guests but I think we may have to install a permanent station in the Quilt Room for my daughter. It's fairly clear she's living her dream and enjoying the heck out of it."

"I think we all are," Marge said. "I have to remind myself every day that this whole thing is for real and that I'm not going to wake up someday in my scrubs and be back on the sixth floor of the hospital in my old nursing unit."

"Even if you have to deal with the Heloises of the world?" Sunnie asked with a grin.

"Even if," Marge said, and focused on the paper in front of her. "Let's see. Where was I? Oh yeah, so Ricky will come in everyday after school and help with miscellaneous chores and then bus tables in the dining room during dinner service. I plan to make the rounds a few times to be sure that housekeeping is staying on top of their chores—vacuuming, dusting, keeping the trash and recycle bins from overflowing, and making sure the Poop Decks are sparkling clean for our guests." Marge flipped to the next page of the stapled printout. "Most of my next two days will be spent setting up the agenda for next week, sending out a final communication to our first week of *paying* quilters, and verifying the details for next month's quilter-in-residence slash speaker."

"Can we spare a few minutes to squeeze in some fun this afternoon and at the same time possibly get H to smile a little bit?" Sunnie raised her eyebrows and rubbed her hands together in a conspiratorial manner.

"Hmmm, I can see you have something in mind. Do tell."

Sunnie perched on the edge of Marge's desk. "I bought, or should I say the retreat bought, two matching Moda Jelly Rolls from the Ship's Store. Last night I cut each of the 44-inch strips in half to make them the length of a fat quarter. That gave me 160 strips that were 22 inches long."

Marge bobbed her head, but wondered where this was going.

"We have forty-eight guests…that's three strips per guest. The perfect amount for…"

"Left-Right-Center!" Marge crowed. "What a great idea for an icebreaker. Too bad we didn't think of this yesterday."

"I know, but the whole purpose of the soft opening was to fine-tune our agenda. I think we should let the ladies know that at…oh, say three o'clock this afternoon, there will be a mandatory activity in the Hannah Brewster Quilting Room. I've asked Andres to set up one of the big round tables with chairs for ten. We'll have five rounds and draw names randomly out of one of those Pilgrim hats Phree bought for props. The five winners will comprise the players for one big final deciding game of winner-take-all."

"You've given this some thought. I'm impressed."

"We can thank cranky-pants Heloise. I just wanted a

fun activity where she *had* to join in. Maybe for a few rare minutes she might let her guard down."

Marge thought Sunnie was being rather naïve if she thought she could get a smile out of that judgmental witch, but didn't say so out loud. Instead she said, "Let's do it. I'll print out some kind of simple invitation that we can pass out at lunch and we should also make some announcements." Even if Heloise groused through the whole thing, the other forty-seven quilters would still have a good time.

The women each fussed at their desks for a few more minutes. Marge checked her e-mails and found that eighteen new registration forms with down payments had come in overnight. She'd need to input the information into the system and send confirmation receipts. Nedra had been doing a fabulous job keeping the schedule updated on their blog and website. They were now looking at the next three weeks at the MQR being completely filled, with the fourth and fifth weeks having only four and two openings, respectively.

"I bet it's going to be odd for you having Wednesday and Thursday off work from now on," Sunnie said. "How are you feeling about not coming in for those two days?"

"Like someone's ripping off my right arm," Marge laughed. "I'll probably stop in for a little fix each day…just a short visit to stay in touch. I'm pretty sure by the third or fourth week I'll be able to tear myself away from here and be happy about the time off. But right now I think it's a good idea to check in." Sensing this might be a good time to talk with Sunnie about Val and the e-mail from her sister, Marge tucked the printout of a spreadsheet inside a color-coded folder as she said, "I'm going to visit my daughter at Northern on Wednesday afternoon. I got a rather panicky call from her this morning and I'm kind of concerned."

"Oh." Sunnie stopped what she was doing and looked up. "What's going on?"

"I'm not really sure. She says she's horribly homesick and wants to come home. As in come home for good."

Marge heard the main door to the retreat open, and within seconds Nedra entered the Bridge at the same time Sunnie said, "Val? We're talking about Val the social butterfly, right?"

"Morning," Nedra said. "Is something going on with Val? Is she okay?"

"Is who okay?" Phree asked as she walked in on the heels of Nedra.

Marge was actually glad to have these other friends join in on the conversation. They both had daughters that had gone away to college and might be able to help with some important insights. "Val phoned me when I was on the way to the retreat this morning and claims to be having trouble with being homesick...apparently very very homesick." She closed her eyes, sighed, and shook her head from side to side as though she could rattle the pieces of this puzzle into place. "I don't know, I'm sure there's more she's not telling me. I can feel it. My mommy radar went through the roof while we were talking." Looking from Phree to Nedra she asked, "Did either of your girls have problems with being homesick when they left for school?" Marge swallowed the dread that had crept into her throat and for a moment she feared her rich breakfast might make a second and very ugly appearance.

"I think Emily felt a tug of homesickness, and only a little tug, the first week she was gone but that was all. Now she can barely find time to call me anymore," Phree said. "How about you, Ned?"

"Lizzie, my oldest, had a little trouble, but I always thought it was more a combination of nose-trouble and jealousy with only a hint of homesickness. That girl was so worried that she was missing out on something her little sister might be getting back home that she couldn't enjoy her first taste of freedom. It took her about two weeks to settle in and after that, she never looked back." Nedra slid an emery file from her purse and with a back-and-forth motion began to smooth her nails. "Allison, who I always thought was a lot like your Val, was comfortable from the first day. To be honest, *I* had more trouble with them leaving home than they did."

Phree prodded Marge, "What makes you think there's more to it?"

"It's just not like her. Two months ago she couldn't wait to get to college and today she was sobbing uncontrollably to come home. Her homesickness shouldn't be this bad. She's been there for six weeks. Heck, I barely heard from her the first two or three weeks she was there." Marge swiveled the chair and grabbed a tissue from a box on her credenza. "It doesn't add up…it just doesn't add up."

"Listen to your inner voice. It usually nags us moms for a reason," Phree said. "Even though decades have passed, our children were still part of our body once and that's a special connection. Mothers just know."

"Let's say for the moment that I *am* overreacting…if she is simply homesick, do I let her come home or should Bud and I play tough-guy roles and make her stick it out? Or is there a middle ground…a compromise of some sort?"

"I for one think it's a good idea that you're going for a visit. You'll be able to sort out a lot of information from being with her for the day," Nedra said. "But don't spend the day making yourself crazy by looking for something that may not be there."

"I've got so many horrible scenarios going through my head that I want to rush out there right now and find out what the heck is going on."

"Hmmm…" Sunnie cocked her head to the side. "Why don't you take tomorrow off and surprise her with an unannounced visit?"

"I…I…I don't know. It seems so…so…" Marge struggled against this being a brilliant idea or a knee-jerk reaction, and knee-jerk reactions were *not* typically Marge's style. "You've got a point. Maybe I should go when she's not expecting me. I could tell her that I was so worried that I switched my day off to get out there as soon as possible—a spur of the moment type thing."

"Figure out what works best and I'll cover for you if you want to take tomorrow off. Don't worry about the MQR."

Phree and Nedra nodded their heads in agreement.

"Oh, look at me," Marge scoffed. "The retreat hasn't even been open two full days and I'm already manipulating my schedule for a day off." Marge stood. "Give me a little time and I'll let you know by this afternoon."

"You got it," Sunnie said.

"Anyway…thanks for the offer to cover for me. I appreciate having the option." The panic Marge had felt only minutes ago still remained. Captain Marge needed a strategy.

"There's nothing worse than not knowing what to do or how to do it when one of our children is in distress," Nedra said.

"You're doing a great job, Mom." Sunnie said. "Hang in there. You'll figure this out." With her signature gesture of support and friendship, she threaded her hand around Marge's arm and said, "Let's stroll through the building and make our charming presence felt among our quilting guests. At the same time we can drop the bomb about plans for some mandatory fun."

"What's this about mandatory fun?" Phree asked.

"Yeah, what gives?" Nedra said. "I think our GMs are keeping secrets from Madam Chairman and their fellow board members."

"Should we tell them or surprise them?" Sunnie pulled Marge closer with a conspiratorial gesture.

"I suppose you'd better fill them in on the plans or we're likely to never hear the end of it."

While Sunnie gave a shortened version of the L-R-C tournament planned for this afternoon, Marge smiled as though she were listening, when in fact she was already mentally driving toward DeKalb where she would comfort her youngest child and only daughter.

Chapter 12
Tim

Tim had taken heat his whole life for being an absentminded egghead professor. He didn't mind the egghead part so much, but he had always found the absentminded term rather insulting. Why couldn't people say *preoccupied* or *intently focused*? Those references sounded so much better and a case could be made in which they actually carried some truth. As head of the American History Department at Sauk Trail Community College, he *was* intently focused on his classes and research. That didn't mean, however, that he didn't or couldn't see past his studious nose. And right now, the worst offender to think this of him was his own wife.

My God, can she possibly think I'm so blissfully confused that I don't even realize something is going on in my own home? This bitter thought had taken root in his mind and Tim was unable to dislodge it.

Maybe it was partially his fault and, yes, he was willing to bear a portion of the responsibility. He had looked the other way for years as the clutter and mess grew while swallowing every last bit of empty space in their home. Last winter the family made a massive effort to rid their home of the excessive choas after Beth's father moved to a retirement community.

For many stressful years prior to that, the disorder had gotten worse day by day as his mother-in-law's terminal illness slowly chipped away at her life. That period of time was followed by Beth's dad requiring daily care and attention due to his ever-present diabetes. Add to the challenge three children, a set of working parents, and eventually something had to take a hit. The Stevensons' Achilles' heel turned out to be housework. A losing battle with clutter claimed their home as an unsafe eyesore.

In true 'Tim fashion' he had researched hoarding, and the information he found wasn't pretty. He discovered that most believe hoarding cannot be cured and typically gets worse with age. Out of compassion he had turned a blind eye when Beth began to stack extra rows of plastic bins in the basement. He was aware that she was saving objects that clearly would have been put in the trash by anyone without a hoarding issue. He told himself she was working it out *her* way and he didn't want to add extra stress to Beth's life by forcing her to do something that filled her with anxiety.

But Tim could see it was clearly time to garner a professional opinion.

Last Friday he had contacted the Counseling Center on campus and left a message with Dr. Colleen Hughes. They had met and worked together around four years ago when Tim needed advice concerning a disruptive student. You could never be too safe with an unruly pupil, and Tim took the safety of all the students in his classroom seriously. Colleen also came to the rescue when his daughter Heather was in need of information about culinary schools.

At this moment Colleen hadn't returned his call, but the beginning of the school year was always hectic and it might take a few more days for her to contact him.

Tim adored his wife from the moment they met. They were soul mates in so many ways yet he didn't want to live knee-deep in clutter ever again and he categorically did not want that lifestyle for their children either.

The question was: Is this a deal breaker?

The answer depended on what, if anything, he discovered as he planned to covertly spy on the activities of his beloved wife this morning during the time he had no classes scheduled.

Chapter 13
Marge

Marge had phoned her husband to alert him about Val and get his opinion on the matter. Together they determined that Marge should switch her day off with Sunnie and get out to DeKalb on Tuesday. They also determined that Marge should give their daughter a heads up that she was arriving a day early. What if she got out there and Val wasn't around, not answering her cell, involved with a class? Marge could easily end up being the one who was surprised.

"I don't want her feeling as though she has to skip classes or miss out on some social plans to hang with her mom," Marge said, aware that if their daughter had been involved with friends, she probably would *not* be horribly homesick.

"Why don't you call her in the morning to tell her you'll be there by one o'clock? That gives her some time to get ready for you but not enough time to cover too many tracks if she's hiding something," Bud suggested.

"Leaving in the morning will also give the two of us time to discuss this in more detail later tonight," Marge added. "Plus help me mentally prepare for the visit and whatever I might find."

"Are you sure you don't want me to go too?"

While Marge desperately wanted her husband to accompany her, she also knew the chance was greater that their daughter would open up more in a one-on-one visit.

She planned to put together a 'care package' for Val. Items from home might help the spirits of a homesick college student and at the same time be something fun they could share. Since school had begun in mid-August, Marge had purchased several new fall sweaters and tops for her daughter; this would be a good time to surprise her with them. After leaving the retreat tonight, she'd visit the grocery store for some of Val's favorite snacks and in the morning bake a fresh batch of cookies. Maybe I'll text Zach and ask him to call her—nothing says 'home sweet home' like a chat with a sibling.

The weight that had been resting on Marge's chest eased a bit as she felt certain this was the best way to handle the situation.

By two forty-five in the afternoon the retreat was abuzz with excitement.

Sunnie, Nedra, Phree, and Marge wandered among the guests in the Brewster Quilting Room. It was fun to see how all of these women, be they stay-at-home moms, professional executives, part-time workers, retirees, grandma's, and anyone in between could be so worked up over an unknown event. Most women typically planned surprises for others and were rarely treated to one themselves. If today's game proved successful, they would definitely be adding this event as a permanent happening to the Mayflower Quilters Retreat weekly schedule.

Names were randomly drawn from the big-buckled Pilgrim hat to indicate who would play which round. The heats were then typed into Nedra's laptop, printed out, and posted by the refreshment area. A rush to the placard ensued as guests hurried to see which round of play they were assigned, and if any new or longtime friends were placed at their table.

"There is so much electricity in the room, you'd think the prize was a million dollars," Nedra whispered to Marge when they caught up to each other.

"And to think that we haven't even announced what's going to take place yet."

Heloise beckoned Marge, and the GM took her time weaving in between stations and commenting to quilters about works in progress. As she approached Heloise's station, Marge could have sworn she saw terror in the woman's eyes. "Yes ma'am, what can I help you with?"

Flustered, H replied, "This whole fiasco is a waste of my time. I won't be play…"

Marge didn't let her finish. "You're playing, so get over it. The success of the game depends on all the guests playing, and we aren't going to let you spoil the fun for everyone else."

"But I don't like…"

"Tough. It's not about you." Marge thought was funny since this was *all* about her. Sunnie had arranged the game as an icebreaker of sorts, hoping Heloise would warm up to some of the other women. Leaning low over H's work, as though she were inspecting it, Marge said, "Try to have fun, but if you can't…fake it."

As Marge walked away she heard an incredulous Heloise say, "Well, I never heard the likes of such a thing."

The first heat of the Left-Right-Center game was about to begin. By 2:55 the players were seated at a large round table and chomping at the bit to get started. Onlookers were three deep behind the chairs—talking, laughing, and nibbling on treats. No one was seated at their stations, not even Heloise. Marge had seen Nedra approach the crabby woman and coax her to join the spectators. She wondered what in the world her friend could have said to convince H to huddle around the table with the other women.

Sunnie announced what they were about to do.

Marge estimated that approximately half of the quilters raised their hands to indicate they had played the game before, many with family members using pennies instead of fabric strips and typically around the holidays. While handing three Jelly Roll strips to each woman, Sunnie continued to relay the instructions of the game, insuring that everyone was on the same page as far as the rules went. There was a general purr of "mmms" when the quilters saw that the prize had to do with one of Moda's yummy new fabric lines. "By the time we're finished with the final round, the winner will be the owner of two full Jelly Rolls."

A chorus of "yays," "woo-hoos," and a few loud whistles rounded out the cheers.

Sunnie called out, "Whose birthday is closest to today?"

It was determined that Janet, who was piecing a Harry Potter quilt for her granddaughter, had a birthday in two weeks. Fluttering a handful of fabric strips above her head like a cheerleader with a pompon, Sunnie sent three dice gliding across the table toward Janet to start the game.

Janet rolled an R (right), a C (center), and a solid dot (keep). She slid a strip to her right, tossed another toward the center of the table, and hugged the last strip to her chest.

Within six rolls, Moe was the first player to have no strips left. She pushed her chair back to exit the game, but all of the women who had previously played L-R-C called out, "No! You still have a chance!"

Sunnie suspended the game to explain the rules again, and the happy guest rejoined the game. By the next round, Moe was rolling the dice again *and* with four strips in front of her.

Marge took time to observe the reactions of both the players and the onlookers, deciding this would be the perfect activity to employ at all future retreats as a means of introducing some fun and camaraderie. When her eyes fell on Heloise, she was shocked to see the normally grumpy woman practically smiling. True, she hadn't joined in with the fist-pumping younger quilters chanting, "Go, go, go." But when the woman standing directly behind H put both hands on her shoulders, shook them, and shouted, "Yay!" H's tentative smile deepened to a toothy grin. Marge spotted Nedra, who had been snapping photos while she circled the event, clicking a picture of Heloise being unusually happy for a change. Her eyes met Marge's and she gave her friend a thumbs up as if to say, "I got it." Later this evening Ned would have the MQR blog updated with photos and a story to reflect the enjoyment of the competition.

Finally, only two women remained. A jumbled pile of precious 2 ½-inch strips rested in the middle of the table. Moe, who only minutes earlier thought she was the first to leave the game, had two pieces in front of her, and her sister Geri had one. Their other sister, Mary, would be in another heat.

The bystanders pumped fists of fabric strips in the air, bobbing in unison and chanting, "Ger-EE! Ger-EE! Ger-EE!" Cupping her hands together, Geri gave the lone die a good long shake. When she spread her fingers apart mid-shake, the die bounced on the table and skittered to a stop. The chanting halted as all heads craned toward the cube to get a better look.

C—Center! Geri covered her face and threw her head back in mock disbelief as the crowd began to clap and cheer, "Moe! Moe! Moe!" The final strip landed in the center and with both arms spread wide to encompass the entire pile, Moe swept the prize into a hug.

Heloise was clapping!

The whole game took less than ten minutes, but the room was transformed into wild excitement and smiles. Not for the first time Marge thought, *Sunnie is a freaking genius.*

The quilters who were designated to play in rounds two, three, and four took their turns and the gathered crowd remained enthusiastic, cheering and chanting and whooping for the players. The coveted fabric strips were draped around the winners' necks and proudly displayed like beautiful Hawaiian leis.

"Ladies!" Sunnie called above the din. "This will be the fifth and last heat before the Winner Takes All Battle. The first

Mayflower Quilters Retreat L-R-C Championship will be held after dinner tonight at eight p.m."

Cheers and hoots punctuated the applause and as Marge joined in by clapping, she wondered how long these women could carry on like this. Sunnie looked her way with a questioning smile on her face and shrugged as if to say, "Who'd have thought?"

Heloise took a seat and primly folded her hands in front of her.

Phree sidled up to Marge and whispered, "What a wild group! I feel like we just went four rounds in the Coliseum. Think it will always be this nutty?"

"I do," Marge answered. "I suspect not many of these women get a chance to let their hair down in their day-to-day lives."

"Good point."

"We've given them permission to go crazy. It's a compliment to the MQR that the passengers are all comfortable enough to slip into the fantasy."

Marge felt her cell phone vibrate in her back pocket. "Excuse me. This might be Kim Diehl. We've been texting today to settle on a date for her Quilter in Residence gig next spring."

Phree waved her off to take care of the message. Marge turned to step aside as her finger traced the code that would unlock her phone. The text was from Val: "Can we move me back home Wednesday? Please. I hate it here." Marge's stomach churned at the same time it plummeted. *Thank goodness I followed Sunnie's suggestion and I'm heading out there tomorrow. Something's very wrong – this isn't like Val.*

The message had rattled Marge, but there was nothing she could do at this point except wait until tomorrow. There was no scenario she could think of where it would be correct to cave in to her daughter's anxiety and allow her to come home for good. Marge knew only too well that Val needed to face and work through whatever was happening, or she would be powerless over her fears in the future.

She also knew that was going to be easier said than done for both of them.

An explosion of cheers brought her back to reality. Chants of, "Ka-THEE! Ka-THEE!" came from the wall of spectators. Marge got back to the circle in time to see the final roll. With three strips to her opponent's one strip, Kathy rolled three Centers and lost the game to none other than Heloise.

"Hel-o-WEEZ! Hel-o-WEEZ!"

Marge would never have believed what happened next if she didn't see it with her own eyes. The crankiest, most cantankerous woman that Marge had ever met swooped over the center pile of fabric strips, lofting them above her head and spreading her arms wide in exhilaration. The tangle of strips freed themselves from each other as they drifted toward the tabletop, engulfing a laughing Heloise as they landed. A roar of approval filled the room and Heloise accepted hugs from nearby quilters.

Incapable of keeping her mind off Val, Marge nonetheless made her way toward the winner of the fifth heat. The crowd was dissipating and sewing machines were beginning to purr around the room. When they met up, Marge put an arm around H and whispered in her ear, "Well now, look who had fun. You're a rock star, Heloise with an H."

Heloise said a quiet, "I admit I haven't had this much fun in years. I'm glad you bullied me into playing."

Marge guffawed, "You're quite the sweet talker, Heloise. And I'm truly happy that you allowed yourself to loosen up enough to have a good time. I bet that doesn't happen too often, does it?"

Sunnie was gathering the five winners together for a group photo and snagged Heloise to join them. Marge watched as the winners stood in a line with colorful fabric strips hanging from their necks and arms locked around each other's backs.

"Sometimes truth is stranger than fiction," Phree said as they both openly gawked at a smiling Heloise. "Any chance Heloise might change her ways for good?"

"Probably not forever," Marge answered, "But I think while she's a part of our little fantasy here, she's going to be a whole new person."

Chapter 14
Val

Staring at the cell phone, Val reread her mother's text for what felt like the hundredth time—"Hang in there. We'll discuss it tomorrow."

We'll discuss it tomorrow? She might as well have told me, 'No.' Doesn't my own mother realize I'm desperate?

Sitting on her lofted bed, she hugged her knees to her chin. It was comforting to remind herself that Mom would be here on Wednesday. Closing her eyes, she visualized her mother holding her, smoothing her hair with her hand, and telling her it would be all right. Mom's citrusy fragrance would be wonderfully comforting and the thought of it made Val want to be home more than ever.

Remembering a trick from long ago when she was a little girl and afraid on her first few sleepovers, Val reached for a tube of her mother's scented hand cream. Oddly, her mom had packed this for her daughter in case she had a bout of homesickness. "Put this on your hands if you miss us back home—rub it in real good. Lie down with your hands by your nose and get nice and cozy. Then all you have to do is close your eyes and breathe in the scent of my love. I'll be right here with you."

Val's breathing steadied as the familiar scent brought her a peaceful security she hadn't felt for weeks. *I only have to make it through two more nights and Mom will be here. Then everything will be okay.*

Chapter 15
Laura

I can't believe that Marge hasn't taken two minutes to get back to me. Laura slammed the lid shut on her tablet after checking her e-mail again and seeing there was nothing from her sister. *Make that my very important sister who has such a busy life that she can't spare a minute for me. There's always someone or something more important than me that she manages to put first.*

It wasn't good enough for Marge to be an oncology specialist and help cancer patients every day—oh no, she had to switch careers and become the general manager of some stupid quilting retreat in the middle of nowhere so she can be with her little Bunco group all day. *She's got plenty of time for her kids and all of her friends, that's for sure—but apparently no time to contact me. Miss I-Have-A-Perfect-Life can't even answer my e-mail or return my calls.*

The more Laura thought about her eldest sister, the angrier she became. And the angrier she became, the more she thought about driving down to the south suburbs and confronting Marge. It was a vicious cycle—a spinning conundrum of which Laura could not let go.

If she doesn't have the courtesy to respond to me by Thursday, I'll get a hold of her Friday morning and let her know that she can't treat me like this anymore.

Chapter 16
Beth

"Come on kids, the bus will be here any second and it isn't going to wait for you," Beth called. The twins pushed her 'morning buttons' every day as though it was some sort of competitive challenge to see which one of them could get the biggest reaction out of her.

"What can possibly take them so long to brush their teeth every day?" she asked Tim as she emptied several uneaten spoonsful of cereal floating in milk and a few crusts of cinnamon toast into the disposal.

Tim boomed out his cut-the-crap, I-mean-business voice. "Joey. Katy. Now!"

Footsteps and giggles thundered down the stairs as the twins attempted to avoid the early-morning wrath of their father.

"Do you think maybe you'll buy it today, Dad?" Joey had already asked this question at least three times during breakfast.

Ever the patient professor, Tim said, "I've told you that I'm only looking today, Joey. I'm going to compare sturdiness and prices, that's all." With a manly thump on the back of his crestfallen son, he added, "Never fear, buddy, the Ping-Pong table will be here before you know it and the Stevensons' Ping-Pong Palace will be opened to all those who desire to test their abilities."

At the sound of the lumbering school bus, Beth said, "Let's go. Your bus is here. Katy, sweater." Handing each child a brown paper bag she added a quick hug with a pat on the shoulders and said, "I love you…have a good day."

Beth's eyes stayed on the yellow bus until each of her children had boarded and the door swung closed. "I'm so happy Heather gets herself up and out of here in the mornings now that she's in college. I suppose there's still hope that the twins will grow up someday too."

"Oh they will, and all too quickly I'm afraid." Tim added, "Since the whole family knows that I'll be Ping-Pong shopping on my half day off, what does your day look like?"

"I've got clients this afternoon and a million errands to run this morning. I'd also like to stop in at Heritage Manor to see Dad for a few minutes…that is if I can squeeze it in."

"Go ahead, babe. Get started on your errands if you want. I can clean up this mess and get the dishwasher going. The Ping-Pong stores don't open till ten." They had taken to calling the four local shops selling the sought after commodity 'Ping-Pong Stores' as though the only items they sold were Ping-Pong related paraphernalia.

Beth panicked. She wanted him out of the house so she could load up the car with more bins for the storage unit. "I…um…that's okay, most of the shops I'm headed to don't open till ten either."

"I'll head down to the basement and see what I can do with some of those bins to get them out of the way."

"NO!" *That was way too loud and obvious.* "I mean I was going to try to work on that today, too. I have some ideas."

Her husband persisted. "Why don't we get this cleaned up and work on the basement together? I thought maybe I'd surprise the kids and see if we can fit in a comfy futon, if there is such a thing as a *comfy* one, and maybe a few of those new style beanbag chairs that are a huge improvement over the kind when we were young. You know, make it cozy for the kids."

Beth felt trapped and she sure as heck didn't want him nosing around the basement until she had dragged all of her bins out of there. Having no other choice she said, "Sure. Let's do it…together."

"You don't seem very excited about me helping you with the project."

If he only knew how un*excited I am.* "I wouldn't say that. I love when we get a chance to work on things together. It rarely happens anymore."

Tim's ringing cell phone broke into the tense conversation and Beth had a few minutes to think. Coming up with an impromptu solution, she would suggest that they take the rare opportunity to visit her father together at Heritage Manor. *I can make this work, and then I'll still have time to get to the storage lock…*

"That was the college," Tim said as he walked back into the room and exhaled a puff of air while he combed a hand over his scruffy locks. "I've got to head over there for a bit. Guess I won't be able to help you after all."

Beth stifled a grin. "Oh, darn." Not even caring why he had been called in on his half day off, she added, "No problem. Go take care of work and I'll get started in the basement."

Bending to brush a kiss on his wife's cheek he said, "It shouldn't take long. When I'm done I'll head straight to the Ping-Pong stores and check out the prices and options."

Barely trusting herself to speak for fear of sounding a little too giddy, Beth finally said, "Sounds good."

And it *did* sound good—really, really good.

The first thing that Beth did when her unsuspecting hubby left was to yank an empty plastic tub from the stack of new bins she had hidden in her salon. She calculated there should be enough time for three, maybe four trips to the locker before her first appointment arrived this afternoon. Stationing the tub on a kitchen chair, she swept newspapers, magazines, weekly sales papers, and a pile of unopened junk mail into the container. With the counters and tabletop clutter free, she brought the bin into the family room and repeated the process with anything she wasn't ready to send to the landfill or recycle. Making their way into the plastic tub were TV Guides, more magazines, and even a small stack of sweaters that Heather had deemed 'out of style' and earmarked for the women's shelter.

I'll go through these someday when I have more time. That little promise had become so familiar to Beth that she repeated it as though it were a prayer and as if on cue, it helped to calm her anxiety. After all, she did the best she could to keep things tidy around their home. So what if every once in a while she took a shortcut by doing a 'power sweep?' And so what if she had a secret storage locker? In the long run everybody could be happy—and she truly did intend to sort through these papers one day. Truly, she did.

After tossing three holey socks of Joey's into the tub, Beth straightened to examine her surroundings. Clutter-free in zero to sixty—it had been easy as pie as she maneuvered tub 'number one' out to her car. Not long after, she backed the red compact SUV down the driveway to make the seven-minute trip to her secret storage unit. The vehicle was stuffed to overflowing with plastic tubs full of her precious belongings. Since there was no need to stop inside the Load 'n' Stow office anymore, she wouldn't have to suffer through a chat with Grandma Twang or Mr. Winker.

Life was good, and it had just gotten better.

After three times to locker number 505, Beth was ready to call it a day. A fourth trip would put her way too close to her first client's appointment. Hands on hips she surveyed the basement where the mythical Ping-Pong table would stand ready for competition. The bins had been drastically reduced in the course of the past two days and she estimated that she had a few more storage locker trips to make. That was good because the locker was filling quickly.

Lifting the covers to get a better look at what exactly was inside each of the clear plastic containers that remained in the basement, Beth made two separate stacks with an invisible dividing line. To anyone else it would simply look like a wall of large bins, but she knew right where the separation began. She would take the tubs on the left to the Load 'n' Stow and the stack on the right would remain—partly as a decoy and partly because they were filled with things that the family needed to access.

Seasonal items such as snowsuits, gloves, mittens, ice skates, and scarves were among the objects on the right-hand side of the pile. Christmas, Easter, and Halloween decorations, along with other holiday fare, also landed on the side to stay put in the basement. There were several tubs of kitchen items that might only be used once or twice a year and a host of tools that Tim rarely used but which needed to be kept handy.

Beth estimated two more trips, three at the most, and the whole job would be finished. Her treasures would be safe, secure, well organized, and out of harm's way. She would have a fresh start trying to control her demons, and *this* time she would succeed.

I may like to save things, but at least I have them organized and I'm also able to avoid discovery from my hubby. There's no good reason to tell him everything I do, is there?

Feeling happy yet duplicitous at the same time, Beth was all too aware that sometimes you just had to do whatever it took to survive.

Chapter 17
Tim

Tim walked across campus to Dr. Colleen Hughes's office not noticing the nippy coolness or the scent of autumn that hitched a ride on a late September breeze. He was too focused on what he would say to Colleen, how much he should tell her, and how exactly he would phrase it. But his biggest struggle was the mixture of guilt and shame that he was about to share an ugly secret concerning his wife. Tim reminded himself again that in order to help Beth he would have to reach out to someone because he certainly didn't have a clue about how or where to start the process.

As soon as the Ping-Pong table had been discussed, plastic bins filled with who-knew-what had been disappearing from the Stevensons' basement at an alarming rate. Tim was confused and felt betrayed by his wife's actions, but he was certain that simply confronting Beth would be a mistake unless he came to the battle armed with some facts along with an effective plan.

Last winter when the family spent several weeks de-cluttering their home, Tim had played the role of the supportive and understanding husband. He now wondered if that had been a mistake. Had he inadvertently enabled Beth to grow more and more devious as he turned a blind eye to what she was doing? Yes, it was a quick fix, and yes it seemed good for the family at the time…but now…now it seemed as though he had given his wife permission to continue to mislead him.

"Thanks for seeing me today, Colleen," Tim said as they shook hands.

"I'm always happy to help a colleague, Tim." Colleen closed the office door behind her for privacy and motioned Tim toward a chair in front of her desk. "Have a seat."

This wouldn't be the first time Colleen Hughes had come to the aid of a Stevenson family member. Last fall when Tim's daughter had cautiously announced that she was interested in pursuing her love of cooking, Colleen made recommendations and connected Heather with a student counselor whom she knew at Joliet Junior College.

As Dr. Hughes walked behind her desk to sit she said, "How's Heather doing at JCC? Has she settled in to college life and the culinary arts?"

Knowing this was simply an attempt at small talk and a way to break the ice, Tim kept it short and said, "Heather's doing great. She loves college and her professors. It turned out to be a perfect fit. Beth and I are grateful for your help."

Colleen put her left palm up to wave his comment away. "It was my pleasure. I've been trying to get culinary arts added to our academic lineup for about three years now. These things take time." Crossing her arms on her desk and leaning slightly forward she said, "Now, what brings you here today?"

Tim did *not* want the whole faculty and staff of Salk Trail Community College discussing his private life, and the guilt of airing less-than-desirable information about Beth made him uncomfortable. "I assume our talk will be confidential?" he speared his hand through his hair again and the knot in his stomach grew.

Nodding with a reassuring smile, Colleen answered, "Absolutely."

"Well," he inhaled a long breath and let it out, "I'll get right to the point. There's someone in our family who I believe has a hoarding problem and I'm not sure what to do or how to help."

"I see," said Dr. Hughes. "Tell me what's going on,

Tim."

Feeling the weight of shame, Tim was uneasy at first sharing details of his wife's behavior, but once he began explaining the situation he felt emboldened that this was the correct course of action. Dr. Hughes was sympathetic and encouraged him to keep talking. It was a relief to finally have someone with whom to discuss the problem and he even opened up and explained how he was in the beginning stages of fearing that if Beth's hoarding and deception could not get under control, that it might possibly drive a permanent wedge between them.

He also confessed that until the good doctor's phone call came through this morning, he had planned to covertly follow Beth with the hope of finding what his wife had done with the missing bins. "I'll have to try that again some other time. She's definitely taking the bins to another location. All I can figure out is the possibility that she has rented a storage locker somewhere."

After finishing the facts of the story he said, "So what I'd like to know is this: What, if anything, can be done to stop or stem hoarding activities, who might be able to help us, and what exactly is the success rate of getting this behavior under control?"

Colleen leaned back in her office chair and with a practiced, calm voice said, "First let me express my sorrow that your family, especially Beth, is experiencing this disorder. I admit that I have very little professional knowledge about hoarding. What I do know is quite rudimentary, mostly from observing a neighbor whose family left him when his hoarding severely affected their safety."

Saddened, Tim shook his head. "I'd like to avoid that at all costs. I believe Beth is close to a tipping point and I'll do whatever it takes to help her and keep our family together. I'm not sure if hoarding is clinically classified as an addiction or a compulsion and I guess that really doesn't matter to me...I just want her and our family to have all the tools available to help fight this demon before it gets any worse."

There was a light rap on the office door and Colleen's receptionist opened it a few inches. "Dr. Hughes, your nine-thirty is here."

"Thank you, Angela. We're almost finished."

Tim started to rise, "I'm sorry I kept you so long."

Motioning with her hand for Tim to sit down she said, "I have a therapist in mind that I think could be helpful. Erin is very well versed in hoarding and OCD issues. Let me make the initial call sometime today and I'll get back to you by this evening or tomorrow. What's the best way to contact you? Phone? E-mail?"

"I'd prefer if you used my cell number. I have late classes today and will be tied up until at least seven o'clock." An edge of embarrassment crept into his voice. "E-mail won't work as I'd rather not have this sensitive issue sent to my office. And if you still have our e-mail address from when you helped us with Heather...well...Beth uses our home account more than I do, so that won't work either. Texting might be a little more discreet. I don't want my wife..."

"I understand."

Tim recited his cell number and said, "I have to be careful. Beth's phone is one digit higher than mine. I wouldn't want to give you the wrong number."

They both stood up at the same time. Tim reached out his hand to shake, but pretty and single Dr. Colleen Hughes grasped it in both of hers, giving it a light squeeze. She held his hand a little too long and gazed into his eyes, eventually saying, "I'm glad you felt comfortable enough to share your concerns with me. And if I can do anything, Tim, anything at all to ease your anxiety," another squeeze, "please don't hesitate to contact me."

Tim felt uncomfortable. All he could do was nod at the woman who was smiling at him with over-white teeth and wouldn't let go of his hand.

Chapter 18
Marge

From the driver's seat of her car, Marge spoke to her husband through the open window. "I hope I have everything."

Bud placed his hands on top of the car door and bent to peer inside. "I can't imagine that we've missed a thing." He reached in and gently massaged the back of his wife's neck. "She'll be fine, hon. Whatever's going on, we'll help her through it."

Marge leaned her cheek to rest against his flannel shirt sleeve. "I know. I just want to hold her in my arms and then I'll feel better."

"Only a few more hours and you two will be together."

Marge had texted Val about an hour ago but hadn't heard from her yet. Eight in the morning was still early for most college students, especially her night-owl daughter. "I'll let you know when I hear something. I'm not going to leave the retreat until eleven. That should get me to DeKalb around one." Marge envisioned taking her daughter to lunch and then out for a mani-pedi. She would bolster Val's spirits with a good dose of love from home. Praying that was all it would take to help her daughter, Marge's gut was telling her a different story and she didn't like the feeling one bit.

"Are you sure you don't want me to go with?"

"I still think it's best for only one of us to go but thanks, I'll be fine. Maybe you can pull duty next time."

"Hang in there, hon. Go have a few pleasant hours at work—it'll get your mind off Val till you can leave." Bud leaned his head inside the open driver's window and kissed his troubled wife on the cheek, straightened, and then lightly smacked the top of the car with one of his hands. "Call me for any reason. I love you."

"Love you, too."

It had been a restless night for Marge and somewhere around five o'clock this morning she gave up the idea of sleep and went to the kitchen to bake a batch of cookies for Val. Even though a fresh tub of buttery Pecan Sandies would not solve anything, Marge took comfort from the fact that she was doing *something*.

By the time she had pulled into the employee parking area at the retreat, Marge had worried herself into a bad place again. *Get control. You'll be there in a few hours. She'll be fine. She's simply homesick. Val would have told you if there was anything else going on.* ...But would she have?

Marge walked past the end of the building, not looking up to admire the painted Friendship Quilt Block as she usually did—today its lovely simplicity held no peace for her worried mother's mind.

"Why in the world are *you* here?" Sunnie stopped what she was doing and practically gaped at the GM as she walked into the Bridge. "I thought you were going to see Val today."

"I am." Marge placed her purse and tote bag in their customary places. "But I'm not leaving until eleven and rather than sit home and worry even more than I already have, I thought I'd spend the time here."

"That's probably a good idea. Any word?"

"Nah."

There was a long pause as Marge sat at her desk, clasped her hands together, and stared ahead at nothing.

Sunnie was there with an arm around her shoulders. "Come on, girl. Let's get some caffeine in you and have a little chat."

"But who will..."

"I'll text Phree and tell her that I need to attend to something in my suite for a few minutes and to keep an eye on things. She's in the dining room having breakfast with Heloise. Apparently our resident 'ex-cranky-pants' is holding court with all of her new best friends and has a whole different attitude after winning the final round of L-R-C last night."

"Seriously?" Marge said.

"You bet, and it's quite a story. I told Heloise I was going to start calling her Miss Phoenix because she rose from the ashes of a miserable attitude and became a happier new person. Wait till you see her. She's having a ball." Sunnie lowered her voice and tilted her head toward Marge as though they might be overheard. "Between you and me, I wonder how long it can possibly last."

"Long enough until she leaves the MQR I hope," Marge said.

"You got that right, sister."

Sunnie's suite was bright and cheerful, much like Sunnie herself. An oversized window that Phree had ordered custom made afforded her mother a lovely perspective overlooking the wooded acres surrounding the retreat. Marge gazed over Phree's roof and across the treetops; her breath caught at the beauty. The trees had only recently begun to change colors with yellow being the predominant color after green. The spectrum of oranges and reds were beginning to show until one day not too far off the trees would stand naked with winter wind blowing through their bare branches.

"What a spectacular view," Marge told her hostess. "And would you look at this?" Centered in front of the window were two mismatched kitchen-type chairs on either side of a small bistro style table-for-two. Each chair was artfully covered with colored images of quilts from what appeared to be magazines. "As I've said many times, you're an artistic genius, Sunnie." Marge ran her fingers along the back of the chair feeling for seams. She found nothing except a silky smooth finish. "The contrast of these whimsical chairs with the changing scenery outside is stunning. It feels like a fantasy."

While Marge ogled the setting, Sunnie brought a carafe of coffee to the table and added fine porcelain cups with saucers. "I agree. It feels like a fantasy to me, too, and I love every minute of my life here." She motioned to a chair. "Sit. I thought this might help your troubled soul. I know it works for me." She followed with a plate of brownies and cookies, saying, "Pilfered from the kitchen late last night long after it was closed to the guests." Sunnie winked. "I'm not above sneaking down there and pinching some leftovers." Pouring coffee she told her friend, "Now sit and center your spirit. If you want to talk, talk…if not, we'll take a meditative thinking break."

Minutes passed.

The beauty of the view, along with the influx of caffeine from rich hot coffee and a thick fudge brownie *did* heighten her mindfulness as well as refresh Marge. She watched a breeze tease hundreds of small yellow leaves from trees and race them along the ground. Finally she spoke after sipping more coffee. "I needed this. Thanks."

Sunnie swirled the last drops of liquid in her cup. "My pleasure. Any time, my friend."

Marge leaned back in her chair and took her eyes from the window. Looking at Sunnie she said, "I'm deathly afraid. I wanted to rush out to NIU and see Val but that would have been wrong on so many levels. Yet on the other hand it seems like maybe I made a terrible mistake by not getting there sooner." Marge paused and pressed her lips together. "*If* Val is homesick, I didn't want to enable her and set precedence by rushing out there." Another pause. "But if my instincts are correct…"

"Leave now." Sunnie placed a hand over Marge's. "You'll get there two hours ahead of when she expects you.

See if she's in her dorm. If she's not, text her or call her. Wait in your car or walk around campus. It's a beautiful fall day. You'll feel better simply by being close to her."

"You know me, Sunnie, I'm usually not like this...actually I'm never like this."

"Then go. Leave now."

Sunnie pushed her chair back from the table and Marge followed suit.

Marge stammered as she started to gather cups and spoons, "Thanks for the...I should help with this..."

Sunnie took the items from Marge's hands and said, "Never mind these things. Go to your daughter and help her."

Chapter 19
Dr. Colleen Hughes

Colleen was fairly sure…no, she was one hundred percent positive that Professor Stevenson had signaled interest in her. She had often wondered how he had gotten saddled with a wife that was a quilting hairdresser and, for the love of God, apparently a hoarder on top of it. No wonder the head of the History Department found his colleague and equal so fascinating.

She had always seen the man to be powerfully attractive with his carefree longish hair and innate genius. She had to admit that his penetrating, all-knowing eyes, which only minutes earlier had looked to her for help, had started to melt her heart in the warmest of ways. Not that she was an expert in such a thing, but his shoulder to hip ratio wasn't bad either.

Sighing, she rose from behind her desk to retrieve the next pathetic student who needed her guidance and counsel to survive yet another semester. She could easily understand how a 'looker' like Tim would be bored to tears with his life and hoping to spice it up a tad. Stopping at a mirror before opening the office door, Colleen took a moment to finger-comb a few stray hairs and admire her perfectly veneered teeth. She stood straighter and pulled her shoulders back. She liked what she saw and she suspected Tim had liked it too.

Maybe I'll make an appointment to have my hair cut and styled by the hoarding quilting wife and get a better picture of the real Mrs. Stevenson. Colleen exhaled a soft unladylike snort. Nah, she probably isn't any better a stylist than she is a wife.

With her hand on the doorknob Colleen smiled and hmfped. This was going to be so easy that Beth Stevenson would never know what hit her.

Chapter 20
Beth

Honey Crisp apple slices dipped in chunky peanut butter alongside a handful of Ruffles potato chips served as Beth's late lunch. The tattered sofa that had long ago been part of the Stevensons' family room now sported a new slipcover and resided in Beth's sewing studio, serving as her favorite place to relax. Often if a client was running late, she would scurry to this magical room next to her salon, put her feet up, and enjoy the serenity that came from simply being around fabric and quilts. Due to the close proximity of the rooms, she could easily hear when a customer entered the shop. Propping her already tired feet up on the sofa, Beth finished eating lunch while reviewing her appointments for the day and checking the computer for updates about the Mayflower Quilters Retreat.

Nedra had been busy posting to the retreat's social media sites and it looked as though the MQR was in full swing. She couldn't wait to hear the inside details of the pictures and stories that she saw on their blog, Facebook, and Twitter pages. The photo that really stopped her was one of Heloise, arms spread wide, head thrown back, and laughing as fabric strips reigned down around her. Where had the idea for an L-R-C tournament come from? Beth thought it was a brilliant idea, but as far as she knew it wasn't even part of the agenda two days ago. She was eager to work her first shift at the Pampered Pilgrim tomorrow and be part of the excitement.

As Beth scrolled through the pictures of the Quilters

Mess Hall for the second time, her computer chimed that a new e-mail had been deposited in her inbox. Switching tabs at the top of her screen to her e-mail account she saw there was a message from GrannyQuilter007. She didn't know or couldn't recall who GrannyQuilter007 might be. The subject line read, "Hi Beth, it's me." So between the quilting reference and whoever it was using her name, she felt comfortable viewing the communiqué. When she clicked to open the new e-mail, a single, all-capitalized word taunted her from the body of the correspondence: HOARDER!!!!

Beth clasped both hands over her mouth. As she drew in a surprised breath, she heard footsteps overhead in the kitchen accompanied by her husband's voice and the lighthearted 1950s sitcom reference he always used.

"Honey, I'm home."

Beth panicked.

Heat rose in her chest, burning with shame and humiliation. *Who would do this to me?* She hated the 'H' word. She was NOT a hoarder.

Hoarders had messy houses filled with mold and smelly trash, where the only place left to walk was on top of piled-up garbage. Hundreds of cats or other pets roamed through junk like a nomadic pack. She envisioned mice and rats and decay when she thought of hoarders. Her family lived in a relatively clean house that was occasionally overrun with clutter, but then again whose home *didn't* suffer from untidiness now and then?

Tim was heading down the stairs! *Crap, I need to pull it together.*

"Hallooo, Beth? You down here?"

She realized she hadn't called out when he announced he was home. In order to hide the offensive e-mail, Beth clicked back to the MQR's blog page. "In here," she called. "I'm in the sewing studio."

Rounding the corner into the room, her husband asked,

"Did you have something to eat yet?"

With her tummy ready to relieve itself of her meager lunch, the last thing Beth wanted was to look at, taste, smell, or even think about food. "Yeah. Sorry. I wasn't sure you'd be back before classes…"

"I wasn't sure either, but I managed to get through that impromptu meeting on campus with plenty of time to complete my research on Ping-Pong tables." Tim paused and scrutinized her. "Are you okay? You look pale."

"Really? No, I'm fine." Trying to sound casual, she laughed and added, "Maybe I'd better get a little makeup on before my customers arrive."

Tim clasped his hands behind his head, stretching muscles that were weary from the great Ping-Pong shopping expedition. His words came out strained from the stretch as he said, "I've got just enough time for a quick sandwich before I head back to campus."

Beth was reminded how good-looking her husband was as his polo shirt rose above the belted jeans he wore and showed his flat stomach. "What was the meeting about?"

"Oh, the usual interdepartmental crap that goes on at colleges. To be honest, I don't know why I even had to be there." He walked closer to Beth as he peered down at the computer screen. "Is that the retreat?"

Swinging her legs off the sofa, she made room for Tim to sit next to her. Patting the seat she said, "Sit. I'll give you a virtual tour of the latest photos Nedra posted."

Tim snugged his wife against his chest as he rested his arm across her shoulders. Images of the Mayflower Quilters Retreat scrolled past with Beth keeping up an animated commentary for her hubby. While many spouses would not want to be bothered viewing a stream of photos about a quilters retreat, Tim was different. Beth didn't know of one thing that would not pique his interest, especially when it came to learning something he knew nothing about. She supposed that was the professor in him—always searching for knowledge and then sharing what he knew through educating.

The truth was that Beth wanted to keep him next to her as long as she could. As a matter of fact, if possible, she'd choose to stay like this forever…snuggled and warm next to her loving husband. Because Beth knew that once Professor Tim Stevenson left the room, she would be uncontrollably compelled to click on that e-mail again and stare at the one word that had shaken her day.

HOARDER!!!!

Chapter 21
Marge

It took miles, many many miles, to leave behind the homes and buildings of suburban Chicago and finally see nothing but farmers' fields. Towns were sparse, but an occasional white two-story homestead with the typical red barn and outbuildings dotted the flat Midwest landscape. This was corn country and being late September the crops had not yet been harvested.

The ubiquitous combines would make their appearance in a few more weeks, crawling over the earth from early morning until late into the night. With high-beamed spotlights guiding their way as they kicked up plumes of dust while moving over the fields like massive mechanical insects reaping, threshing, and winnowing the crops. DeKalb corn signs could be seen at the edges of most fields and those fields started as close to Interstate 88 as possible.

Needing to pay close attention to the demanding traffic coming and going from Chicagoland had taken Marge's mind away from her daughter for the first portion of the drive. Once reaching the mind-numbing boredom of the flatland her thoughts careened back to worry mode. It was closing in on eleven thirty when she entered DeKalb city limits. It would only take a short time to reach campus and the building that housed her daughter's dorm room.

Marge still hadn't heard from Val and that added to her concerns. She would skip the walk around campus, the stop she had planned at the university bookstore, and the hunt for an ever-present Starbucks. Instead, she would head directly to

Val's room on the off chance she might be there.

Chapter 22
Val

Lifting her head from the NIU trash can, Val swiped at her mouth with the edge of a crusty T-shirt sleeve. She remembered the day her parents had helped set up her room at college and then taken her on a shopping spree at the campus bookstore. After collecting all of the textbooks for her fall classes, Mom and Dad had combed through the store while stuffing binders, T-shirts, and other paraphernalia with NIU logos into the already full shopping cart.

"You'll need one of these trash cans," her father had said. "You know, show your school pride. Go Huskies."

Val was humiliated that the cute guy in the next aisle might have overheard the lame comments. With a tch of her tongue Val rolled her eyes, snatching the can from her father's hands. "We've already got enough junk. Let's get out of here."

Val desperately wanted to leave the campus bookstore without being any more embarrassed than she already was. *Will they never leave?* Turning on her heel, she headed toward the checkout. In the long line Val stood with her back to her parents. For several minutes, she maintained an I'm-not-with-these-old-people coolness while clutching the damn trash can that she didn't even want.

"Honey?" her mom said softly and tapped her on the shoulder. "We're almost done here and then Dad and I will take off and let you settle in. But I just want to check if you have enough flash drives for your computer?"

Spinning to face the two people who loved her more than anyone in the world, who were simply trying to help her, who were excited for her, who were footing the bill for her education, she saw such sadness and pain in their eyes that she winced. But not knowing what to do, Val dug in with a shoulder slump and a breathless and sarcastic, "Yes, Mother. I've got it covered."

But today, as she hugged the Husky wastebasket waiting for the next wave of nausea and vomiting to come and finally subside, all she could think about was the pain she had witnessed in her parents' eyes because of her own self-centered cruelty. It made her cry. And gag. And vomit. And wish…how she wished for that silly moment back so she could erase her ungrateful and self-centered actions. Valerie Russell had changed in a matter of weeks and couldn't wait to feel safe in her parents' loving arms again. Never to let them go.

She must have fallen asleep after toppling over on her bed during a relentless surge of dry heaves, unwilling to let go of the security of the trash can. At one point she vaguely recalled her roommate entering for a few minutes and gathering supplies for her next class or something.

When Mary spotted Val she mumbled, "Gross. It stinks in here." Then she said, "Whatever." And was gone.

The nausea had subsided and the crying jag had diminished to the point of a few stray tears. Left feeling exhausted, Val promised she'd never put herself through this again. She felt like a helpless observer of her own life and recognized that tomorrow would not be any different. Closing her eyes and allowing herself to doze, she dared not move for fear that the cycle might start all over. There were a few hours before Mom would arrive and she wanted to rest before seeing her. She still had time to take a fast shower and make herself presentable by one o'clock. Maybe Mom wouldn't put two and two together and figure out what she'd been up to.

Some sort of hideous steady tapping brought Val to a

half-awake groggy state. What the hell was that noise? After a short while it registered and she froze in place with fear.

Her mother was at the door.

"Val, are you in there? It's me...it's Mom, honey. Open up."

Chapter 23
Beth

HOARDER!!!!

Who the hell is GrannyQuilter007 and why did they send me that horrible e-mail? Who knew this specific detail about her private life or, she should say, *thought* they knew because again—she was *not* a hoarder. This was nothing but downright meanness on someone's part. Sadly she couldn't even share the message with anyone because she felt so damned ashamed, and embarrassed, and terribly horribly guilty.

Beth snipped, clipped, dyed, blow-dried, sprayed, endlessly smiled, and chatted with her customers as she silently promised herself that this time tomorrow her life would be different. A change *would* take place. It had to. No more collecting things.

'Tomorrow' had been her secret refrain for what seemed like forever, a hymn of sorts as she prayed for help to start her life anew. No more would she surrender to her anxiety. She would fight it; she was tough. No more would the frightening question, "What if I need this item sometime in the future?" control her life or mind. She could win this battle. She would be strong.

She would be strong.

She would be strong.

She would be strong—right after she moved the remainder of her bins to the storage unit for safekeeping before going to the MQR for her Wednesday salon gig.

Longtime client Carol Halvorsen had been keeping up a mostly one-way stream of conversation about the recent birth of her first grandchild when Beth felt her cell phone vibrate again in her hip pocket. Each time she had slyly taken a peek to make sure it wasn't an important message from the kids' school, or her hubby, or her father at the retirement community. And each time it had been a delete-worthy piece of cyber junk mail or a nonessential phone call she could return later. But this time her phone had pulsed three times in a row and she was eager to see what was going on.

There were only a few moments until she would move Carol from the styling chair to sit under the beehive hair dryer in order to speed up the hair-dyeing process. At that point Beth planned to go to the back room and check any messages, e-mails, or missed calls. In order not to seem too rude, she needed to focus on what Carol was saying, make a few appropriate comments, but most of all stay calm.

"Let me know if you need anything." Beth was like a mother tucking a child into bed as she settled her client under the dryer. "I'll be in the back room for a few minutes shelving a box of products."

"No problem. I love the warm coziness and white noise of this thing," Carol said. "I'll probably doze off in a few minutes."

Beth wasn't four steps away from the hair dryer when she had her cell phone in hand tapping in the security code. The notification bar told her there were no text messages, but three new e-mails. She tapped the logo of the white envelope with a red M and a list of e-mails filled the screen. What she hoped to see was easily delete-able garbage or a message from one of her Bunco Club friends. The last three e-mails she received were all from the same sender, and Beth felt her heartbeat quicken at the same time her skin went damp.

The source of the e-mails was the same: GrannyQuilter007.

So acute was her focus that Beth's peripheral vison disappeared as she experienced a case of tunnel vision. The only thing she could see clearly was the screen on her cell phone as she tapped on the third e-mail from the top—that would be the first one sent.

3:06 pm: "It won't be long and your children will hate you."

3:09 pm: "It won't be long before your husband leaves you."

3:14 pm: "Get ready, Beth. The exodus has already started."

Beth stood trembling with helplessness and anger while awash in heart-pounding anxiety. She heaved herself toward the sink and vomited. *The exodus has already started.* What exactly did that mean? And who the hell was doing this to her?

In what used to be the safe cocoon of her home and her salon at 3:26 and 3:28 pm her phone notified her of two more e-mails. Each once simply read: HOARDER!!!!

Beth felt she might be sick again as she grasped that she was being stalked.

Chapter 24
Marge

Collecting her thoughts, Marge paused for a few moments on a bench outside of Val's residence hall. Resting next to her was an oversized tote bag filled with offerings for a homesick college student. After arriving on campus, Marge had texted her daughter for the second time today. Assuming Val would get back to her immediately, she had sent: "Surprise! I'm here, honey. Couldn't wait till 1:00 to see you so I came a little early."

But the surprise was on Marge. By the time she had walked to the residence hall, no word had yet arrived from Val.

With her eyes locked on the main door of the twelve-story building in the off chance that Val might show up, Marge watched as students came and went. She was pondering what a wonderful oasis college is in the scheme of life when a familiar girl caught her eye. It wasn't Val, but if Marge was correct, she thought it was her daughter's roommate. *What was her name? What was her name? Something simple and old fashioned. Annie? Ann? Maryann? Mary!*

The girl had already passed by but was only about ten feet away when Marge called out, "Mary!"

Bingo! The girl turned, looking for whoever had said her name.

Marge stood and approached the student, who had gone stock still. "Hi, Mary. I don't know if you remember me but I'm Val's mother. We met on move-in day."

Recognition dawned. "Hi, Mrs. Russell," Mary smiled, and her smile quickly turned to dread. The girl seemed uncomfortable and started to back away. "I...uh gotta get going. I'm meeting someone at the student center." Mary nodded her head toward the direction of Holmes.

"I won't keep you," Marge said and noted that Mary was as jittery as a June bug. "Have you seen Val lately? Do you happen to know if she might be in your room?"

"I, um...yeah, I just came from there. But, um..." Mary's shoulders slumped in defeat as she gave up the ruse and said, "I just left the room and she was there."

"Is she okay?"

"I think you'd better get up there as quick as you can."

Marge reached out, seizing the girl's forearm, and whispered a hoarse, "Thank you." Turning on her heel, Marge took off like a rabbit. She was nearly to the door when she heard, "Mrs. Russell."

Marge spun toward the voice and saw Mary hurrying forward with the tote bag of goodies.

"You left this on the bench."

The elevator ride to the eighth floor felt endless as students entered and departed the stuffy and smelly unadorned box at every floor. Most of the youngsters were quiet and somber but several of the girls were giggly and gossipy. At last the number on the indicator flashed eight. When the door opened, Marge was the only person to get off. Three boys bumped into each other to get around her before the doors closed. Marge hurried past them but not until she heard one of them say, "Shit, dude. It's going up."

In only a matter of steps she'd be at her daughter's room. Sick at heart from Mary's comment to rush up to the room as fast as she could, Marge lengthened her stride. She reached room 632 and tapped lightly. Nothing. Turning the knob quietly, she found the door was locked. Tapping a little louder, Marge said, "Val, are you in there?" More tapping and still nothing. "It's me...it's Mom, honey."

This time when Marge knocked, her voice grew higher and louder. "Open up."

Listening for sound through the thick door, she thought she heard movement inside the room. There it was again. In a firm I-am-your-mother voice, Marge brooked no nonsense. "Val, open the door. Now."

The lock on the handle clicked open and the doorknob turned. Marge gasped and took one step back in horror. The ghoulish apparition in front of her surely could not be the same beautiful young woman she had left in this very room six weeks ago. Could it? Stench wafted into the hall and in a questioning voice she asked, "Val? Valerie Russell?"

Val let go of the door and threw herself at her mother, sobbing like a small child, "Mom…oh, Mom, I'm sorry. I'm so sorry."

Marge held her daughter, engulfing her baby with protective hugs while she purred loving sweetness close to her ear. Val continued to sob and apologize with no sign of stopping as Marge guided them both inside the room and shut the door behind them. Her daughter would not let go or loosen her grip. This near-feral young woman looked like a stranger but was indeed her precious Val.

Fearing meth or heroine might be involved, the nurse in Marge took over. In a matter of seconds she mentally ticked off visual symptoms, hoping to make some kind of preliminary diagnosis or at the very least an intelligent guess. Eyes: bloodshot with dark circles. Face: puffy, swollen, and red. Smell: stale vomit and unwashed body. Hair: stringy, also unwashed. Clothes: filthy, crusty. Weight: down, breasts larger. …Breasts larger?

There it was.

Marge feared she had her diagnosis and it had nothing to do with drugs.

Chapter 25
Beth

Beth was combing out and blow-drying Judy, her last client of the day. She had disregarded any vibrating notifications from her phone and once she knew that the twins were safely home from school, she had placed her cell phone out of reach. Ignorance was bliss, and right now Beth could be the poster girl for that saying. The angst that had been burning through her chest was somewhat extinguished without the constant reminder of messages arriving. Lesson learned: leave the cell phone at arm's length until this stalker person stopped tormenting her.

Unsnapping the cape from Judy's neck, Beth swung it away from her body and gave it a slight shake, allowing the leftover cuttings of snowy white hair to trickle to the floor.

"As usual, I love it," Judy said. "Thanks, Beth, it's just what I wanted."

"You're very welcome, my dear. With your cruise falling on our usual date, shall we set your next appointment for...let's say six weeks?"

As Beth took care of the details and goodbyes to Judy, all she could think of was a cold Dr. Pepper and her cell phone. Her final client of the day reached for the door handle and Beth heard heavy footsteps hurrying down the stairs. It sounded like Tim.

If he was planning on snooping around the basement or fooling in the Ping-Pong area he wasn't going to find much. She didn't need this right now. She wanted to get to her cell phone and see if any other offensive e-mails had arrived. For

God sake, couldn't she even have five minutes to herself?

A light tap was followed by her husband squeezing his head through the barely opened door. "Excuse me." He was being polite in case customers were present, but when his eyes scanned the room and saw only Beth he opened the door and walked in.

This was all very unusual.

"Everyone gone?"

"Yeah the last person just left. What's up?"

"We got a call from Heritage Manor. They've been trying to reach your cell."

Beth's hands flew to her face, covering her mouth and cheeks. Something must be wrong with Dad.

"It's George. He took a tumble from his wheelchair and hit his head." Tim moved toward her and placed a hand on each of her shoulders. "He seems to be fine, but as a precautionary measure they brought him to the hospital to be checked out."

"I…I…I need to…"

Tim took over. "I'll lock the door and close up down here. Hit the bathroom and get your jacket and purse. Don't forget your cell."

"Do you think he's really okay? You don't think he…and they aren't telling us, do you?" Beth left the 'D' word out of the sentence. She couldn't say it.

"No, I think he's fine…I really do. I talked with Betty from the Manor. You know how much she likes George. Her voice was normal and it didn't sound as though she was upset."

Tim had taken care to lock the door leading outside and turn off the lights throughout the salon while Beth gathered items she would need. She walked in front of him as he flipped the final switch, throwing the salon into darkness.

"Heather's going to be home studying tonight so she'll see that Katy and Joey have dinner and get them in bed on time. She knows what's going on, but I haven't told the twins."

The reality of the whole day collided head on with Beth as Heather met her with a hug at the top of the stairs.

"Grandpa's going to be okay, Mom."

Beth felt the pull of tears at the back of her throat before they escaped from her eyes.

"We should go," Tim said as he picked up car keys from the counter.

Her daughter released her after a final squeeze. "Be sure to tell Grandpa I love him."

Chapter 26
Val

Her mother's clean citrus scent smelled like home to Val and being held in those safe, familiar arms felt like love. It was a wish come true. This was where Val needed to be right now and where she wanted to stay forever—sheltered, protected, and most of all cherished. Over the past several weeks she had lost her way and was no longer sure of herself. With her footing askew, she had been unable to regain confidence in who she was or where she was headed. But simply the scent and touch from her loving mother had sparked hope in her confused heart.

Aware that Mom had guided her into the privacy of the dorm room and then closed the door so they were away from curious stares, Val was allowed the luxury of clinging and weeping until she was spent. Mom stroked the tangled and oily mass of matted hair with continued coos, caresses, and kisses which had finally stemmed her crying. Marge had accomplished a successful one-handed Kleenex search through her dangling purse and then dabbed the dampening squares at her daughter's cheeks. Her mother broke the embrace, put an arm around her shoulder and said, "Val, honey, what in the world is going on here?"

Val detected pity in her mom's gaze, watching as her knowing eyes checked out unwashed hair and wrinkled and stained clothes. But right now she'd take pity—she'd even take anger if that was the price she'd have to pay to have her family's love and support.

"Are you okay? Will you share with me what's

happened? I love you, sweetheart. You know you can tell me anything."

At the sound of her mom's caring voice, a fresh wave of emotions gripped the frightened girl as more tears threatened to fall. Not sure where to begin the nightmare of the past six weeks, Val said nothing; she wasn't ready to fess up to what she had done, so she stared at the floor and shook her head. Clinging to her mother, she was hopeful she'd never be forced to let go.

Help me, Mom. I'm so scared and I don't know what to do.

"Look at me, Val."

Mom was firm, causing Val to burrow deeper into her shoulder. *Don't let me go. Take me home. Get me out of here and maybe this will just go away.*

"Valerie. It's going to be all right, sweetie. I'm here. Dad and I love you. It's okay."

Her mom was being patient and soon Val quieted again.

"Do you want to go home? We can leave right now."

An eruption of runny mucus bubbled from her nose and Val snuffled out her first words almost hysterically. Swiping the back of her hand under her dripping nose, she said, "Yes…take me home, please!"

"This is what we're going to do, honey," Marge said and steered the two of them to Val's rumpled bed. "First I want you to take a shower and wash your hair. It will make you feel better. While you're in the shower, I'll gather up all of your clothes and school books and anything else you need. We'll load the car and head for home. We can stop and get a sandwich or burger to eat on the way."

Another citrusy embrace from her mother left Val weak in the knees with the growing desire to get away from this place as fast as possible. A shower sounded good, but the thought of being home and sleeping in her own bed motivated her to cooperate with her mother's plans.

"We'll sort things out, baby. It'll be okay. Dad and I will take care of you. We love you so much."

Her mother fussed and patted and finally led her toward the bathroom and the shower. "Let's get going, okay?"

Reluctant to let go of her mother's hand and with red eyes and wet cheeks, Val expressed her biggest fear and begged, "Please don't leave without me."

Chapter 27
Marge

It was easy to see that Val was shattered and broken. This was not the same girl that Marge and her husband had delivered to the NIU campus only six weeks ago. After hearing water running in the shower, she broke for the window and heaved it open. The smell in the room was sour and stale but it was nothing compared to the odor that emanated from her daughter's clothes and body.

Tapping her cell phone, she called Bud as she tugged the fitted corners of the bottom bed linen free from Val's bed. In the seconds she waited for Bud to answer, Marge picked through discarded items on the floor and tossed familiar articles of her daughter's clothing onto the discolored sheet. She planned to pile as much as she could onto the makeshift tarp, bundle it up, tie it like the bandana of a hobo's bindlestick, and somehow get it to the car. After that she would load up the two stained pillow cases. She was hopeful there might be some stray garbage bags she could snag for everything else.

Bud answered his cell.

"I can't talk long. Val's in the shower," Marge told him. "She's in pretty bad shape."

"Has she been hurt? Did somebody…"

"I'm not sure but I don't think so. She hasn't been taking care of herself. Something must have happened to prompt it, but she hasn't told me anything yet. All she's done is cry and hold on to me since I got here. I'm hoping she'll open up on the drive home."

Marge wasn't sure if it was a good idea to share her suspicions about their daughter over the phone. But at this point she figured it best if Bud had some time to think about the possibilities of an unexpected pregnancy. Resting only for a moment at the desk chair, she combed her fingers through her hair, formed the words in her mind, and said, "I've got no proof of this, Bud, and as I told you Val's not talking…but I've got a gut feeling about what's at the root of this." Pausing for a beat Marge exhaled, "I think Val might be pregnant."

"Oh God." Her husband moaned a mournful sound, and Marge recognized the lament as the end of many dreams they had shared for their daughter. "My poor girl. I pray you're wrong."

"So do I." Marge rose. With the phone clasped tight between her ear and shoulder, Marge continued to dig through the detritus of her daughter's room and gather pertinent items.

"When do you think you'll get here?"

"I should be done gathering all this crap up about the time Val finishes with her shower and dries her hair. Then I have to get it down to the car…"

"Don't kill yourself, Marge. If needed, I can drive out there in the next few days and pick up everything else. Just get her home as quick as you can."

"I might take you up on that." Marge scanned the room and decided to take some clothes and Val's computer…screw the rest. "I want to get some food in her. The plan is to make a quick stop for carryout and eat on the road. If traffic doesn't become an issue, I'm guessing we'll be back between four thirty and five."

"Is there anything I can do on this end to help?" Bud asked.

Marge had mentally run down a laundry list of items in her head. After Val had left for college, Marge personally de-cluttered Val's room and then washed, folded, and put away any stray clothes that had been left behind after the chaotic exodus. The sheets on the bed had been washed and changed, ready for a visit at the drop of a hat. The bathroom that Val and Zach shared had been scoured, supplied with clean towels and was unused since the kids had both gone to college in August. The only thing they might need was food, but there was enough at home that they could throw together a decent meal or even order out if Val wanted something special. Standing straight, Marge rolled her shoulders and flexed them until her back made a slight cracking sound. "Yeah, there's something you can do."

"What's that?" Bud sounded eager to walk to the ends of the earth if it would help their child.

"Start praying."

Chapter 28
Beth

Guilt had tormented Beth on the drive to the hospital. *I should have visited Dad more often instead of spending so much time hiding things from Tim. Maybe if I had taken the time to visit today like I said I was going to, this wouldn't have happened. What if Dad didn't really fall, but instead is being abused by some staff member somehow…someway? I'll never forgive myself.* Around and around these thoughts swirled until they had burned a white-hot hole of blame deep into Beth's soul.

Tim guided his befuddled wife through the double doors that opened automatically into the hospital. The unique 'hospital smell' overwhelmed them; filling their lungs. Holding tight to her husband's hand, Beth prayed the Manor had told the truth when they said George was okay. She asked Tim again, "They said he was fine, right…and that bringing him here was only for precautionary measures?"

"Hang in there for a few more minutes and we'll be able to see for ourselves."

As they approached the information desk, Tim told the white-haired volunteer behind the counter, "We're here to see George Munro."

The friendly helper handed Tim two blue paper passes stamped with today's date and directed them to the Intensive Care Unit, room number 318. Beth took this as a good sign that her father was still alive but he *had* hit his head—what quality of life might greet them? Bewildered and unable to relax until she finally saw Dad with her own eyes, Beth walked toward the elevators in a daze.

Once in the intensive care unit they passed several

rooms. Sleeping or unconscious patients lie on beds with metal side-rails, connected to clear tubing and beeping machines—some with tearful family members holding tight to the limp hand of their loved one. Beth's eyes began to fill with sorrowful tears—tears of regret and guilt at the thought of how she would miss her father if he didn't make it through this ordeal.

Turning the corner in the ICU, they saw a long stretch of rooms with empty beds as they made their way toward the last room. *Why had Dad been isolated so far away from the nurse's station and the other patients?* There appeared to be something going on in her father's room. A nurse stood facing the door with her back to their approach, and Beth watched the RN's shoulders shaking as though she were crying uncontrollably. They were still too far down the hall to hear anything, but Tim squeezed her hand and then let go of it as he slipped an arm around her shoulders and drew her near.

Oh my God, he must be in real bad shape. Maybe I'm too late! Beth let her tears fall freely, making no attempt to hide her emotions.

Last February when Dad opted to move to an active retirement community, he had hoped to give his overwhelmed daughter a break from being his sole caregiver. Heritage Manor had been a perfect fit for George. He had a handicap-accessible apartment with a lovely view and an active social life within the community, enjoying countless events and frequent overnight bus trips. He even had a girlfriend named Daisy. Beth's father was 'living the dream' and Beth had finally found time to focus on her family, friends, business, and a secret, ever-growing collection of items.

The nurse turned and walked toward them.

Beth expected to see the woman dabbing at cheeks wet with moisture. Instead, an ear-to-ear smile split her face and she was laughing. *She has the nerve to laugh as my father is struggling for his life...how dare she!* They all three stopped about five feet from room 318 and faced each other.

"I'm George Munro's daughter, Beth Stevenson. Can you tell me anything about my father's condition before we see him?"

The grinning nurse ran her tongue over her lips forcing the inappropriate gaiety into a more somber frame of mind. "Of course, Mrs. Stevenson. Let's go somewhere private so we can talk. Follow me, please."

Chapter 29
Marge

Taking her husband's advice, Marge cut back on the rubble she had accumulated to what could easily be handled in three trips to the car. If Val was not returning to NIU, Bud could drive his truck to DeKalb, load it up, and be home in a few short hours. While Marge made her way down in the elevator and back up to the room three times schlepping paraphernalia to the car, she advised her daughter to lie on the bed and rest. Val looked pale and weak, and Marge didn't want her overextending what little strength she had.

After picking up sandwiches at Subway, they were finally on the road heading toward Whitney. When Val wasn't staring out the window, she nibbled slowly at her lunch. Marge estimated she had eaten about half of a six-inch turkey Sub, a whole bag of chips, a large chocolate chip cookie, and a bottle of water. This made the mother in Marge happy, but very little conversation had passed between the two of them—certainly nothing of consequence.

Rolling up the remainder of the sandwich in the green and white paper, Val said, "Thanks, Mom. That was good."

Marge wanted to ask what seemed like a hundred questions, but instead she said, "Why don't you lay your head back and see if you can get some sleep. You look tired."

In the silent car, void of music or radio, Val did as her mother suggested. Turning her face toward the side window, the exhausted girl closed her eyes and was breathing slowly within minutes. Marge reached above the gap between the two seats and lightly touched her daughter's hair. Over the past several hours Nurse Marge had observed enough and felt certain her little one was expecting. *Oh, precious daughter, what are we going to do?*

Farmhouses, barns, and the utterly flat landscape was broken up with an occasional small town as the silver SUV made its way toward the Russell home. In her mind Marge replayed how difficult life had been when she was a child and what madness transpired when she showed up pregnant at sixteen-years-old.

Living with irrational, argumentative parents and an alcoholic and physically abusive father, she had been hungry for affection and friendship. Her father would never agree to allow 'strange' children to enter his home, and that included a menagerie of neighborhood kids. On the flip side, Dad also didn't allow his daughters to step foot in anyone else's home. "You never know what's going on behind closed doors or what kind of gossip some nosey bitch is going to pry out of you."

Marge didn't know why Daddy was so worried about closed doors...*they* shut their doors so why was it wrong if their neighbors also shut theirs? She knew what gossip was but Marge didn't think she knew any that might need to be pried out of her. In addition, she wasn't aware of any nosey bitches around the neighborhood...everybody's mothers seemed real nice.

Marge was permitted to play outdoors only when school was out for the summer, and she could travel freely anywhere up and down her block. When Mom called or Dad whistled, she had to hightail it back home as fast as possible to avoid Dad getting mad and coming after her. It still made Marge sick when she thought of her father lashing her bone-thin body with his belt and then torturing her mind with his acid tongue.

Little Marge Parker had ached for a girlfriend, a *real* girlfriend—someone with whom she could play, share secrets, and talk about little girl dreams. Debbie Kowalski was as close as she would ever come to fulfilling the role of a true girlfriend. Debbie lived four houses from her on the other side of the street, and the summer before first grade they were fast friends. Skipping to Debbie's house after breakfast, Marge played all day in the sun and fresh air. Mommy was busy with the new baby and didn't have a lot of time to play anymore. That was okay. Marge was a big girl now and she was going to be in first grade when summer was over. Debbie and she planned to sit next to each other all day long in school—they could even walk there and back together. The summer days were usually warm and long. Rainstorms came and blew past rather quickly, but occasionally lasted a whole boring day. That's when Marge would beg her mother to let Debbie come over to play inside.

Mom was always firm. "Your father will be very mad at both of us if she steps in this house."

That was all Marge needed to hear to remind her to obey the rules.

Val stirred, shifting from her right side to her left in the passenger seat but never opening her eyes. It was good she was getting some rest.

Marge's thoughts shifted back to 'the summer I had a friend.' The incident lived as a clear reminder of living with evil. The girls had constructed a house on Debbie's expansive back porch using frayed clotheslines tied to porch posts as a foundation which supported walls fabricated from blankets and sheets. The 'walls' were clipped into place with Mrs. Kowalski's snapper clothespins.

Debbie's mother was so nice to them. She had delivered a huge cardboard box of old clothes to the girls so they could play dress-up. The dresses were so fancy and they all smelled of different flowery perfumes. There were even high-heeled shoes in the bottom of the box. Debbie dove into the jumble and came up with a small cedar box sporting a colorful vacation-like painting on the lid.

"Makeup!" she squealed.

The girls each held onto the box and jumped up and down, pigtails flying at the sides of Debbie's head and Marge's ponytail bouncing at the back of her neck. Marge had never played house with real makeup before and couldn't wait to see how beautiful she'd look after they dressed up. She was certain Mrs. Kowalski must be the fanciest and nicest person she had ever met in her whole life—and she secretly wished that this fancy lady was her own mommy.

"Maybe we can spend the night in our playhouse tonight," Debbie said. "Sometimes when it's real hot inside Daddy drags a mattress out here so we can sleep where it's a whole bunch cooler."

"I wish I could but I don't think my daddy would let me do that," Marge said. A funny sensation came over her—all prickly and hot and she felt as though she had been a bad girl just by wanting to spend the night. She didn't know why she felt bad…after all she was having fun wearing Mrs. Kowalski's pretty dress and fancy high-heels.

The girls lifted up their dresses so they didn't trip over the hems as they shuffled across the wooden porch in oversized shoes. Marge wore a stunningly beautiful hat with netting that hung down over her face and she was positive it just had to make her carefully applied makeup even prettier.

Debbie's mother brought the Polaroid Land Camera out of the house and helped the girls pose like fashion models. She took two pictures and said that one was for Marge to take home.

The girls started spinning to make their skirts flare out high above their pedal pushers. The higher their skirts rose, the faster they spun and the dizzier they got. Soon their feet became tangled in the high heels they were wearing and the shoes were discarded. The dizzier the girls became, the louder they giggled and squealed until they grabbed for each other. Laughing, they woozily stumbled to the ground where they laughed some more.

It had been the most perfect day of Marge Parker's life. She finally knew what it was like to have a best friend…until. She heard him before she saw him.

"Margurite! Where the hell are you?"

Marge scrambled out of the playhouse so fast she popped a few clothespins and a blanket-wall crumbled to the porch.

"I'm here, Daddy. Right here."

He was only a house away from the Kowalski's.

She turned to Debbie. Ripping at the dress-up clothes she said, "I gotta go."

"Why? What's wrong? I thought we were going to sleep in our house tonight." Debbie had apparently not heard Jake Parker growling for his daughter. Even if she had, she wouldn't have had a clue as to what might happen next—it was beyond her life experience.

One look at his daughter and Marge's father was livid. "What's been going on around here? What's that shit on your face? Are you trying to be a slut behind my back?"

Marge had no idea what a slut was, but she knew it couldn't be something nice if he was this mad about it. "No, Daddy, we've just been playing dress-up." He was close enough that she could smell his breath. He'd been drinking. That usually meant he'd find something to be mad about and then find someone to yell at and eventually hurt. Since Mommy had just had the new baby he'd been leaving her alone, making Marge the only target for his meanness.

Mrs. Kowalski pushed aside several blanket walls and seemed to pop out of nowhere. "What's going on out here? Is there a problem, Mr. Parker?"

"Are you responsible for my daughter's slutty behavior?"

Doris Kowalski's eyes became large orbs and her eyebrows shot into her forehead as she slapped a hand over her heart. "I beg your pardon, sir, that's entirely inappropriate language to be using around young girls. Deborah, get in the house."

"I tell you what's inappropriate," Daddy said. "Letting my daughter dress in these whorish clothes and wear makeup. What are you, some kind of madam for little girls?"

Mrs. Kowalski gasped. "Get out of here before I call the police…you…you horrible man." Her eyes flickered to Marge and she said in a softer voice, "Are you okay, honey?"

Marge's face was wet with tears and she nodded her head. Somehow in the commotion she had been able to remove the pretty dress. It rested in a puddle around her feet. But she had forgotten that the delicate hat was still resting on her head and bobby-pinned to her hair. Daddy grabbed it in one of his beefy hands, crushing it and pulling it off his daughter's head at the same time. Clumps of hair that had anchored the hat with hairpins came off with the veiled hat.

Marge screamed at the pain, and faster than lightning her father backhanded her across the mouth. "I'll give you something to scream about, you little slut."

Marge's head flew backwards and the momentum knocked her to the ground.

Mrs. Kowalski shrieked, started down the stairs toward Marge, and shouted, "Stop that, you asshole. She just a little girl."

Marge 'crab crawled' away from him as fast as she could until she finally bumped up against the decorative underpinning of the porch. Her hand went to her cheek, covering the red-hot imprint of her father's hand. She was out of breath and her head hurt.

"Mind your own business, bitch. This is all your fault." Looking at Marge crying on the ground he said, "Don't you *ever* and I mean *ever* come here again. If you do I'll find out about it and you know what will happen." Bending over his daughter's bruised body and broken spirit, Jake Parker, the man who was supposed to protect his family, jerked her up by one arm until her feet were dangling in the air. He roughly stood her on the sidewalk, barking, "Let's go." He stomped off ahead of her.

Marge looked back at a pale Mrs. Kowalski, who had both hands crossed at her neck in horror. Turning to catch up with her father who was grumbling and cursing under his breath, Marge felt for the back pocket of her pedal pushers. She smiled through her tears and bruises. The Polaroid photograph of Debbie and her was safe.

Another layer of dignity had been stripped away from Marge's self-worth. Soon there would be nothing left. At that point she would be forced to accept the fact that she was simply a bad little girl.

The Kowalskis moved away when the children were in fourth grade, but Marge and Debbie never spoke with each other after that day. Marge still had the photo of two little girls with toothy smiles, arms around each other, dressed in dated castoff garments, with Marge wearing that ridiculous netted hat and a strand of Pop Beads that reached past her waist—a smiling, giggling, happy little girl.

What would Marge Parker's life have been like if happiness would had been the norm?

Chapter 30
Beth

Engrossed in the story about George Munro's fall, five of Beth's friends had stopped what they were working on in the Bridge and listened with concern.

"Oh my God! Is he okay?" Sunnie asked.

"What happened?" Phree said. "How did he fall?"

"You're not going to believe this," Beth laughed. "Nurse Ratched led Tim and I to a small private room and closed the door. Of course, I don't have to tell you that by this time I was near hysteria and had him inches from his last breath."

"Understandable," Lettie said.

"The nurse started by telling us: 'Mr. Munro asked if I would explain to you what caused his fall so he wouldn't have to go into detail himself.' Again, I assumed the worst and thought he must be too weak to talk. I was dumbfounded that this ignorant woman didn't have the common sense to stop smiling. I mean come on, this is serious stuff. 'Mr. Munro was in a hurry to get into bed and apparently the brakes on his wheelchair were not engaged.' At this point I'm thinking *poor guy must have been really tired,* but I said, 'That's odd he never forgets about the brakes. Could he be suffering from dementia?' "

Nedra moaned, "Oh, no! Your dad is one of the most energetic seniors I know."

"He's energetic all right," Beth laughed. "Apparently his girlfriend, Daisy, was in an even bigger hurry to get into bed than Dad and she's the one who didn't set the brakes."

Beth watched as one by one the women understood what had happened to George. Their faces showed emotions of disbelief and humor with a touch of the ewww factor.

"Yep, you got it," Beth said. "Dad and Daisy were doing the nasty. Boinking. Making whoopee. Getting a little afternoon delight."

"I'm afraid that's going to leave a permanent scar on my brain," Phree said.

"Tell me about it," Beth groaned. "And trust me, this is *not* the way a child wants to picture their parent at any age." Shaking off another smile, Beth became serious. "The bump on the head truly was nothing. It was minor and there isn't even a bruise. Apparently they put him in ICU largely due to his age and I'm guessing also because of his disability. They simply wanted to keep a close watch on him for twenty-four hours. He'll be discharged this afternoon sometime."

"If you need to be there, Beth, I can explain to your clients and we can reschedule all of your Pampered Pilgrim appointments for tomorrow," Sunnie said.

"No. Tim will be finished with classes by then and he'll buzz by the hospital to help." Beth shook her head. "Dad sure had us going for a while. It was a frightening hour or so."

"I can't even imagine," Lettie said.

"Well, ladies, I'm off to the salon but I think I'm going to steal a few minutes in the quilting room and see what beauties our guests have been creating. I feel that if I can't be getting any sewing done myself, at least I can enjoy watching everyone else's progress."

"Make sure to check out Andrea's work. She's been piecing blocks for a Dear Jane quilt for several months and she told me she's determined to leave here with all of the blocks finished. Her fabrics are incredible. It makes me want to take the plunge and start one myself," said Phree.

"Got it," Beth said. "Keep me posted if you hear any updates about Val."

It was unnerving to Beth that the only information they had from Marge was a text sent yesterday afternoon to Sunnie that said, "I'm bringing her home. It's bad." Even though the women were all eager to help the Russells if needed, they discussed that it was best at this point to give the family some space.

"I almost forgot to tell you," Sunnie said. "I asked Evelyn to send a plate of scones to the Pampered Pilgrim for you and your clients this afternoon."

"Perfect," Beth called over her shoulder, and then thought, 'Hmmm, maybe I'll keep them all for myself.'

As Beth bent over Andrea's quilt for a closer look, she felt her phone vibrate. Not wanting to be rude, she fought the temptation to peek at the screen. She had received three e-mails early this morning from the relentless GrannyQuilter007. Each e-mail mentioned hoarding, with the last one suggesting that her husband had a 'wandering eye' and that her children were unhappy. Beth still had no idea who could be behind the communiques but they were beginning to unravel her.

Should I share them with Tim? While she would be humiliated for her husband to read them, he was the only person she'd even consider showing them to. *But what if Tim* did *have a wandering eye? What if he* was *unhappy with their marriage?* Beth didn't think he was cheating but as the saying goes…the wife is always the last to know.

Andrea was staring at her. Apparently she was waiting for a reply to a statement or question that Beth hadn't heard.

Stammering, Beth attempted to wiggle out of the uncomfortable situation. "Um, well, this is awkward," Beth said and contorted her face to express her embarrassment, "but I was so intrigued with your beautiful Dear Jane blocks…I…well, I didn't even hear what you said. I'm so sorry."

"No problem," Andrea told her. "I do that all the time too. I get so wrapped up trying to see if I can figure out how the blocks were pieced or how the rows line up that I'm off somewhere in my own little quilty world."

"Exactly!" Beth reached out and touched Andrea's arm as though they were kindred spirits. "Whew, I'm so glad you understand."

"I understand perfectly," Andrea said. "It's a quilter thing."

It turned out that the meticulous piecer of the Dear Jane quilt had an appointment with Beth at the Pampered Pilgrim this afternoon for a new 'do.' "I have no idea what I want. I just know I want something completely new and a little bit edgy." The slender forty-something shared that her husband had left her six months ago and their divorce would be final next month. "Our daughter is staying with him while I'm at the retreat this week. When he brings Olivia home Sunday night, I want to look smokin' hot."

"We can do smokin' hot," Beth laughed. "Sounds like fun."

And it did sound like fun—a whole lot better than dwelling on her own problems.

With a smile still on her face, Beth left the Hannah Brewster Quilting Room and headed toward the Pampered Pilgrim Salon. She had passed through the entryway, where her comfortable shoes squeaked as she walked over the marble floor. Approaching the Mess Hall, her cell phone vibrated again. Beth turned to the right and made her way to the nearest Poop Deck. The washroom was far enough from the main action of the retreat and, as she had guessed, was empty. Slipping her phone from her pocket, Beth leaned against the granite countertop with her back to the mirror.

A notification told her that nine new e-mails were waiting in her inbox: two were garbage, one was from Tim, and six were from her stalker. She deleted the garbage, opened Tim's to find that he had purchased the Ping-Pong table and accessories during a long break between classes and could he come to the retreat and swap cars with her so they could get the thing home? "I don't need to come inside. I'll just take the SUV and leave my pathetically small car for you to drive home." Beth smiled at this—it was so Tim.

Her finger hovered over the first e-mail from GrannyQuilter007. *No. I won't look at these. I'll talk to Tim tonight. He needs to know.*

Beth closed her phone and left the antiseptic smell of the washroom.

Chapter 31
Marge

Bernard 'Bud' Russell had met his wife and daughter in the driveway yesterday when they returned home from DeKalb. He took Val in his arms. The tearful scene that had played out earlier in the afternoon when Marge arrived at NIU was repeated, but this time between father and daughter.

Plans were hastily made to order carryout from a local restaurant. Marge started the washing machine and into it placed the first of what seemed to be an endless heap of stinky clothes. Bud carried various items to Val's room, and she took a long, hot bath after dinner. No one pressed Val for information and she offered very little in the way of conversation. She kept repeating phrases like, "It's so good to be home." "I never want to go back there." "I'm so happy to be with both of you."

Val fell asleep on the sofa with Bud's arm around her shoulders while holding her mother's hand as the three pretended to watch American Pickers reruns on television. By nine p.m. Marge and Bud had tucked their exhausted child into bed and within an hour, the equally exhausted parents were also calling it a night.

After placing a hot cup of coffee in front of her daughter, Marge said, "Good morning, sweetie." In a lame attempt to get the girl talking again, she asked, "How'd you sleep?"

"Better than I have in weeks."

Silence.

"Can I get you some breakfast?"

"No. My stomach..." Val stopped but Marge could easily fill in the blanks: My stomach is upset. I feel like I might throw up.

"Crackers might help. Have you tried eating some?"

Val shook her head. "I didn't know about that."

Marge opened the cabinet where she kept the Saltines. Crinkling waxed paper was the only sound in the room as she unwrapped the soda crackers. Placing seven or eight of the dry, pale squares on a paper napkin, she slid the offering across the table to Val. "Give this a try. It used to help me when...when I felt nauseous."

Observing the crackers as though they were a precious antique, Val kept her eyes lowered.

"Can we talk?" Marge's voice neared a whisper.

It was a moment before Val nodded her head but when she did, tears started their slow slide down her face.

"Will you tell me what happened? I'd like to help."

Again the pause and then the nod.

This time Marge waited. She had all day.

Val nibbled a cracker. "I think that..." She started to speak twice but stopped. "I'm pretty sure that..."

Marge was reminded of a similar moment in her life when she was on the opposite end of this scenario. Teetering between reality and fantasy at sixteen, she knew she was pregnant yet pretended she was wrong about the diagnosis as she fervently hoped the whole mess would go away...disappear...poof.

Jake Parker had slammed his fist on the table and hovered over her so close that the sickening odor of cigarettes mixed with booze had gagged her as it wafted from his breath. Marge had fisted her hand and put it to her mouth, pressing hard to keep the bile at bay. "Say it!" he yelled. "Tell me who the son of a bitch is. Say it! Tell me his name!"

Marge never told.

That night she feared she might lose her baby, and several weeks later blotchy bruises still covered her body from her father's unrelenting attempt to get her to speak. Knowing Dad would hit her either way, she would not give up the name of the one person who had been decent to her…who proclaimed he loved her.

She recalled the feel of blood dripping from her nose and the metallic taste it left in her mouth. But she would not talk. Mom had tried to pull him off but each time she got slapped for her efforts. The next day Marge was on a train for California and an extended visit to help her 'sick' aunt. Many years later, Kim and Laura would tell her how they had huddled together that night in their bedroom, under a blanket with hands over ears while crying for the safety of their big sister.

Marge vowed Val would not be forced, as she herself had been, to do anything she didn't want to. She would give her daughter the gift of deciding what was best for her and her baby. Marge would not offer opinions that might scare or sway Val…years from now, she didn't want her child to feel as though she had been coerced into a decision.

Marge asked, "Did you know the boy?"

Instead of looking up, Val hung her head lower which caused her tears to puddle on the table near the remaining crackers. She finally nodded, yes.

"Did he force you?"

Still there was no eye contact or speaking, but a slight headshake of 'no.'

It was slow going and painful but they were getting somewhere.

Marge reached to cover her daughter's hand with both of hers. "I guess we can assume that you're going to have a baby. I can also tell you from firsthand experience that contrary to what you're feeling right now, it is *not* the end of the world."

Val sobbed once and Marge squeezed her hand.

"I suspect I pretty much know most of what is going through your mind right now and I can assure you that Dad and I don't hate you. I can also promise that we will help you with whatever decisions you make. This needs to be your choice. We won't make it for you or tell you what to do."

Val finally spoke. "But…but that's just it, Mom…I don't have any clue what to do. I only know I wish it never happened." And she added the one thing she had thought over and over from the moment she had verified her pregnancy, "I'm so stupid. How could I have been so stupid?"

"Do you want to tell me about it?"

"NO! It's too embarrassing."

"Honey, I have a pretty good idea how someone gets pregnant," Marge chuckled. "You can leave that part out. What I'd like to know…" *How could she phrase this and not sound accusatory?* "I'd like to know several things. Let's start with—was it just once or were you seeing each other regularly?" *If I can just get her talking…*

"We had been seeing each other from the first day of classes."

"He was in one of your classes?"

Val shook her head. "Not exactly. He was a year ahead of me in Whitney High and I sort of had a crush on him in high school. I don't think you ever met him. We kind of bumped into each other at a party the first weekend at Northern and hit it off."

Only through the sheer force of self-control Marge held back a moan. *I will not press for a name… I will not press for a name.* "Does he know?"

A head shake. "No one knows."

We'll cross that bridge later. "How far along are you?"

A shoulder shrug but still no eye contact. "Maybe four or five weeks."

"I'm going to make an appointment with Doc Josie. We'll see if she can fit you in today or tomorrow." This was the one area where Marge *would* force the issue and insist on routine OB/GYN visits. But Val was a smart girl and nodded her agreement right away.

A beat passed and Marge heard the clothes dryer make a familiar clicking noise. The vibrating sound halted. The silence felt deafening and awkward.

"I'm sorry, Mom. I'm really really sorry. I feel like such a stupid idiot. I just…I didn't think…"

Marge lifted a hand off her daughter's and raised it palm toward Val, the universal sign for 'stop.' "Lest you have already forgotten, might I remind you that about a year ago you learned I had given birth to your half-brother when I was only sixteen? I'll never forget how graciously you handled the news." Unwanted moisture filled her eyes and Marge willed the tears to retreat. "Woman to woman, mother to daughter, I'm here to repay that kindness."

Val covered her face with both hands and her shoulders shook.

Oh no, that's not the reaction I was looking for!

Marge removed her daughter's hands and was shocked at what she saw. Val's face was split with a huge smile and she was laughing!

Confused, Marge said, "What…what the…"

"Seriously, Mom…*lest*? Did you really just say, '*Lest* I had forgotten?' When were you born— in the Dark Ages?"

Marge started laughing along with her daughter. She soon snorted causing both of the women to laugh even harder. Marge moved behind Val, who was sitting in the kitchen chair, and wrapped her arms firmly around her daughter. Val hugged tight to her mother's loving arms. Through the joyful sound of her child's laughter Marge allowed her tears to flow. Somewhere inside this body she held so close lived an echo of the 'Old Val.' Marge knew at that moment her daughter would make it through this ordeal and just like Marge herself had, she would emerge a stronger woman because of it.

Marge whispered in her child's ear, "Lest you ever

wonder, my dear girl, remember that I will always love you."

Chapter 32
Tim

Tim and the twins grunted and pushed as they coaxed the boxed-up Ping-Pong table through the front door of their home. Unopened, the carton was way too heavy and ungainly to maneuver down the basement stairs, so the three Stevensons uncrated the monstrosity in the living room. Tim wielded the box cutter while Joey and Katy carried metal parts and other pieces toward the kitchen, leaning the larger items against the countertops. Clutter spilled into the dining room, littering the house with cut-up cardboard, stray plastic sheeting, and what seemed like miles of brown packing paper. Tim intentionally cut the cardboard into unusable random pieces and planned to have all the trash in the recycle bin before Beth came home to claim it.

Obviously Tim had not factored in the details of transporting a large nine-foot-long and five-foot-wide tabletop down a flight of stairs. Thank goodness the table itself was divided into two pieces.

"Good job, Joey. Don't go too fast. We're almost there." Leading the way down the steps, Tim carried most of the weight while Joey bent low and guided the last of the two big pieces from above. "Okay, I just stepped on the floor. Only a few more stairs, Joey, and the worst part will be over."

Katy followed the procession hoisting a set of unwieldy silver metal legs with locking wheels on one end. As soon as she had deposited the H-shaped item, she bolted back upstairs for the final set. Tim called after her, "Good work, Katy."

She called over her shoulder, "Thanks, Dad."

With a manly thump on his son's back, Tim said, "Gotta say you were the man tonight, buddy. We couldn't have gotten this thing down here without you." The educator and father in Tim knew how to motivate through praise. He also knew that the next thing he had to tell them would not be considered good news.

As they were regrouping and organizing the various pieces that had been hastily deposited around the room, Tim said, "It's almost six o'clock, guys. I really think it's too late to start assembling this thing tonight."

There were the expected groans and complaints from both of the kids.

Tim's phone chimed that he had a notification, but he didn't look at it. "Heather should be home soon. We still have to clean up the mess upstairs and get some dinner in us. I suspect you also might have some homework."

More groans.

"We'll get a fresh start tomorrow after school. That should give us plenty of time to finish the job." The sound of a door closing and footsteps overhead signaled that someone was home and Tim called out, "We're down here."

"I've got dinner," Heather answered. "Mom texted me what to pick up. She said she was running a little late and that she might stay and eat at the retreat. She said to go ahead and start dinner without her."

"Let's get some grub," Tim told the twins. "After dinner I'll clean up the mess upstairs and you guys can get your homework started."

The twins raced up the stairs, poking each other to get to the kitchen first. Following much slower, Tim checked his phone for messages. He had one from Colleen and he stopped halfway up the steps to read it: "I have some info for you but I forgot the folder at home. Have students until 7:30. Meet me at 865 W. 216th Street at 8:00."

Tim wasn't sure where that address was and thought it

seemed a bit odd to meet off campus, but he was eager to receive Colleen's information. Not giving it much thought, he tapped a return message on the keyboard: "See you then."

"Come on, Dad. Let's eat!"

Tim flipped off the light switch at the top of the stairs. The Stevensons Ping-Pong Palace would have to wait a little longer.

Chapter 33
Beth

Andrea's makeover hairdo took longer than the time allotted, but she definitely looked smokin' hot by the time Beth had completed the entire process.

"I can't wait for that two-timing creep to drop off Olivia on Sunday night." Andrea smiled as she held a hand mirror to see the back of her head while poking and smoothing individual hairs with her other hand. "He's going to be shocked out of his itty bitty mind."

Beth had used a deep, rich brown and then added gold and red highlights to transform the all-wrong, home-dyed, ashy color which Andrea had worn for years. The new colors were a perfect complement to Andrea's pale, clear skin. The women settled on a style from one of the brand new glamour magazines in the shop, and Beth continued to tweak the angles and modify the style until her client's cheekbones were accentuated and her prominent nose was deemphasized.

The delighted customer had shown her appreciation with a lavish tip and asked if there was any way that Beth could be her stylist moving forward. "We're both local," Andrea had said. "I'm only twenty-five minutes away in Lansing."

As much as Beth liked this woman and would have loved to have her as a client, she explained as politely as she could that she already had a full schedule and at the moment couldn't possibly take on any new clients.

"Is there a wait list?" Andrea asked. "At the very least *please* put me on the wait list."

Beth feared the woman might cry.

"How about if I call you when I have a cancellation or possibly a last-minute opening here at the Pampered Pilgrim? I'm sure I won't always be booked solid at the retreat." After today's agenda Beth was not sure about this. It did however give her a tactful way out of this awkward situation.

"That sounds doable," Andrea said.

She finally ushered her new friend out of the salon at six fifteen and promised to sit with her in the Mess Hall for dinner. Overall, Beth was pretty proud of the new creation and had enjoyed spending the extra time talking with Andrea. They had even taken before-and-after photos to post on the retreat's blog and Facebook pages.

The intensity of all the decision making and camaraderie the two women had shared this afternoon had undeniably kept Beth's mind off of the increasing number of messages she was receiving from her mysterious stalker. With the workday over and finally alone in the salon for the first time in hours, Beth counted, but didn't open, the messages from her stalker. There were eleven in all.

Riding an adrenaline high from a successful first day at the Pampered Pilgrim, Beth made the decision that she would talk with Tim about GrannyQuilter007 tonight. *Maybe I need to get the truth about this troublesome stalker off of my chest, and while I'm at it fess up about a few other things.*

Chapter 34
Marge

"I have to go back to work at the retreat tomorrow." Marge carried a laundry basket filled with a final load of miscellaneous items still warm from the dryer and set it on the ottoman in the family room. She then sat in the overstuffed chair, retrieving a bath towel from the basket and letting it rest on her lap while she waited for a reply. After she folded this basket, Marge would finally be caught up with all of the extra laundry they had brought home from college as well as this last basket from Bud and her.

Val did not respond. She sat with her eyes focused at some insignificant point beyond the picture window. A stiff breeze swirled yellow and brown leaves and mounded them up against the curb in the street while school buses carrying children back home rumbled past.

Marge had succeeded in securing an OB appointment with Doc Josie for earlier this afternoon. "I can't believe your timing, Mrs. Russell," the telephone receptionist had said. "My last phone call was a cancellation for 1:30 today. Would you be able to make that?"

Can we make it? Marge wanted to reach over the phone wires and hug the woman. "Yes, we'll be there."

The family room remained still, and Marge plunged into the basket for another piece of clothing. Shredded paper sprinkled off the T-shirt. *One of us must have had a tissue or paper in a pocket. Darn, now I'll have to get the vacuum out and...* Marge halted and studied the snips and then softly snorted. What had been such a big deal and had upset her so much only a few days ago lay in front of her. Washed, dried, tattered, and completely forgotten was Laura's nasty e-mail—the e-mail which Marge hadn't thought of since the moment her daughter needed her.

Shaking the tiny pieces from the T-shirt like confetti and then folding it, Marge smiled at the way life had given her a reality check: important vs self-centered silliness…not too hard to grasp this one! She'd vacuum the letter and stay focused on her daughter—on love rather than her sister's wrath.

"Val?"

Peeling her eyes from the window, Val blinked twice and looked at her mother. "Huh?"

Marge would have loved nothing more than to know what her daughter was thinking, but the truth was that because of her own personal experience she felt she had a pretty good idea of Val's thought process.

"I have to go back to work tomorrow, honey." The T-shirt now folded and free from bits of paper, rested on Marge's lap.

"Oh. Okay." Eyes back to the window.

"Can we talk? Is there anything I can do?"

Eventually Val's head moved with several small shakes and dry-eyed she finally looked at her mother and said, "You can tell me what to do."

"That's not for me to decide, babe. This has to be your decision. I'm not going to tell you what to do."

Marge had lived through the other side of this situation forty years earlier and still resented her father's brutal determination that she hand her baby over to a total stranger. She could not presume to know what her daughter should do under similar conditions. Marge felt pride that she would not, could not tell her child which path to take.

Val looked confused and wounded. She stood. "Whatever." And then headed for her room.

"Wait…"

Val kept walking.

"What the...for crying out loud come back here. We have to talk."

Val spun around in the hallway. "Talk about what, Mom? You just said you're not going to tell me what to do. I might as well talk to the third grader across the street—maybe she'd give me some ideas." Val stopped and glared at Marge. "If I knew you weren't going to help I could have just stayed at school and kept hoping this was all some sort of horrible nightmare instead of aching to be back home where you would help me."

Marge was speechless. She stared at her girl. She had given Val a gift, one that Marge herself had desired all those years ago but never received. *Doesn't she understand how precious this is? The gift to make up her own mind – to spread out all of the options, mull them over, and decide for herself? Not to feel hogtied, beaten, or manipulated by a drunken son of a ...*

"Mom?"

Apparently it was Marge's turn to sit slack-jawed and stare at nothing while her daughter wondered what in the world was going on.

Walking toward her mother, she said, "You're mad at me, aren't you? You must hate me for what I did. I've ruined everything...I've ruined my life!"

"No, honey...I don't hate you. Not at all. How could you even..."

"Mooomm, I just asked you what I should do and you basically told me to figure it out for myself."

"No! No, I didn't...I'd never leave you hanging like that." This was not at all going the way Marge had intended. Not even close. "There's been a miscommunication or a misunderstanding here. It's gotten out of hand."

Val hung her head and bit her thumbnail. "I'm confused and scared and I don't know what to do. I need your help...I *want* your help. Dad's too."

Marge tipped her daughter's head up by lifting her

chin so they were looking at each other eye to eye. "Let's start over and get this straightened out, okay?" She smiled. "I'm glad you came home."

"I just want to feel safe again."

"Then that's where we'll begin."

Marge and Bud huddled close together on the sofa in their family room. The volume on the television was just loud enough to muffle their voices if Val should wake up and attempt to eavesdrop. A large bowl of freshly popped and buttered popcorn rested on Bud's lap and within easy reach sat a filled wineglass for Marge along with a Chicago brewed Goose Island 312 beer for Bud. The wood fire blazed bright orange in the fireplace where it crackled and popped, muscling the late evening chill from the room.

"She's exhausted," Marge told her husband, "both physically and emotionally."

"I can understand that."

"I think the confirmation from Doc Josie made it painfully official for her. Prior to that she could pretend her self-diagnosis might be nothing more than a mistake and the problem would simply go away."

"Poor kid," Bud exhaled. "That's quite a load to have been carrying by herself. No wonder she's drained."

"Yes, it is." Marge knew only too well the weight of their daughter's burden. "Let me give you a quick rundown from the OB."

"Sounds like a good place to start."

"The pregnancy was obviously confirmed and she appears to be in her sixth week with an approximate due date of May 8."

Bud nodded his head and spoke around the popcorn in his mouth. "Maybe a Mother's Day baby for our baby."

"Could be." But what Marge didn't say was, "That is if she keeps it." Snagging a handful of popcorn, Marge placed one piece at a time in her mouth and continued. "Doc did an ultrasound and everything seems to be fine. It's a little too early to tell the sex…but at this point I'm not sure Val wants to know." Marge shrugged to indicate that there was so much up in the air right now. "Val's weight is low and we suspect anemia but we'll know more tomorrow when the blood work comes back. In the meantime, Doc started her on pregnancy vitamins which she should be taking anyway." Marge washed down the popcorn with a generous sip of wine. "That's about it for the doctor's appointment. I think Val was overwhelmed. Everything became very real to her."

Bud patted his wife's leg. "She was lucky to have you there."

"I'd like to be able to say, 'It was my pleasure'…but this certainly isn't what we had planned for her."

"No, it's not what we had planned…but we'll all survive this and someday when we hold our grandchild it won't matter a bit." After a swig of beer he added. "We'll all wonder what the big fuss was about."

Marge thought, not for the first time, that she had married the kindest man alive.

They sat in silence for several moments, munching popcorn side by side as they each gazed at the glowing fire and finished their beverages. Bud broke the quiet when he stood and headed to the kitchen with the empties. "Refill?"

Marge nodded and said, "You bet." She let her focus drift away from Val's dilemma. She needed to cleanse her mind and allow it to wander to a happy place…even if only for a few minutes. She thought of the retreat and how much she had missed it these past two days. It occurred to her that she really loved working at the MQR and her thoughts rambled onward to quilting. She was surprised when she realized that she hadn't sat behind her machine or picked up any handwork in weeks.

That's what I need…creative time with a pile of quilty projects. The smell of new fabric fresh from the bolt, its wonderful feel as she smoothed out the folds with the palm of her hand, the sight of a fabric pile of complementary colors ready for cutting to start a new quilt, and the scent of freshly pressed cotton still hot and steamy from the iron. These were some of the things she missed…some of the things she *needed* right now to ease her soul and feel whole again.

"Here we go." Bud came back to the sofa and placed the wine bottle, empty wineglass, and two more 312s on the coffee table. He poured Marge's wine and walked toward the fireplace. After choosing two good-sized logs from the pile stacked next to the hearth, Bud pitched the wood expertly into the cavity of the fireplace where a spray of orange sparkles flew up the chimney. When he had finished his manly duty by poking the firewood into place, he turned to Marge and asked, "So where are we? Do we have any idea what she's thinking yet?"

"No, she's airtight on that subject. Actually she's talking very little about anything. I can't get much out of her." Marge told Bud about the misunderstanding that occurred earlier in the day. "I was so sure I was doing the right thing by not imposing my opinions on her. After what my dad had done to me, I thought there was only one correct way for a parent to proceed. I had blinders on and couldn't see that what Val needs might be entirely different from what I needed."

"The difference is you are helping her out of love. She's used to that. That's what she's known her whole life and she needs that loving help now." Bud put his arm around his wife. "You never felt loved. You were not helped, Marge. You were demoralized into doing something by someone you didn't respect. Val respects you and your input is important to her."

"I see that now, but how could I have been so blind to my daughter's needs… I incorrectly assumed I know everything just because I experienced a similar circumstance."

"To start with, you can stop beating yourself up. You

told me the two of you cleared the air after the incident and had a good talk—so you learned something about yourself and I can guarantee you that Val learned many new lessons from the mix-up." Bud took a long draft from his beer bottle.

"You're right...and, as always, thanks for yanking me back on track," Marge said, in the friendly way of their relationship. "It did finally get us talking."

"Where does all this go from here? Do you have *any* guesses or feelings what direction she might be headed?"

"To start with, she looked horrified when the doctor asked her if she wanted to terminate the pregnancy. As happy as I was about that, I kept a blank expression on my face. You know my opinion on the subject and so does she, but I wonder if she has thought it through. I don't want her changing her mind when she's farther along. The risks become greater the longer she waits."

"Let's assume she knows her own mind on the subject and for the time being not think about this option anymore. Do you know if she's planning to keep the baby or is adoption on the table?"

"My guess is, and this is simply a guess, that she wants to keep it but doesn't know how it could possibly work. I'm not pressing for the boy's name but since he's local, it will probably come to a head at some point."

Bud nodded. "So after the big 'misunderstanding' did you end up offering her any advice?"

"Yeah. I told her that for now I thought she should just chill at home until she feels stronger and the nausea passes. She's more likely to make the correct decision once she feels better." Marge shook and swirled the bowl of popcorn to force any unpopped kernels to the bottom. "To be honest, I'm more concerned that somehow she can get back on track with college. Both Val and the baby will fare better if she has an education."

"I definitely agree with that," Bud said. "Do you think it would help if we had a daddy/daughter dinner date? She's always been a daddy's girl. Maybe she'd open up. And if not, well then we'll have had a nice evening together."

"I think that's a great idea, Bud." And then Marge laughed. "I'm surprised I didn't think of it myself. Mothers and daughters have a way of butting heads sometimes. ...But Val's always had a huge soft spot for her daddy."

"And her daddy feels the same way about his little girl."

Chapter 35
Tim

From his parked car, Tim double-checked the address on the text message that Dr. Hughes had sent him earlier. Tapping his phone off, he stared across the street at the rather nondescript townhouse that, indeed, was at 865 W. 216th Street. *What the heck was going on?* When Colleen gave him the address, he assumed their meeting place would be anything from a coffee shop to a neighborhood bar…but certainly not a private home.

This doesn't feel right. He wasn't sure what troubled him about the situation but Tim's every instinct told him to bolt.

Several minutes passed as he contemplated what to do. The blinds were closed but he occasionally saw shadows as someone walked around in the lit room. Maybe there are other people in there and she isn't alone after all. Maybe I'm simply being paranoid. It was probably an honest mistake and Colleen had forgotten the folder on her kitchen counter this morning just like she had told him.

Tim was the last person who had any right to pass judgment on a forgetful memory. He was constantly forgetting things he was supposed to bring to work. Last week he had left a stack of graded essays sitting on the coffee table in the family room. He had to turn around and go back home when he discovered they were not in his briefcase.

For God's sake, what do I think she's going to do…seduce me? Tim snorted and began to open the car door but paused, remembering how the young, single doctor had looked at him the other day in her office and also how she had grasped his hand.

There it was again. His gut was telling him walking into that townhouse was not a good idea. *Damn.* He had really wanted to get the information and contacts about hoarding that Colleen had allegedly collected for him. He was feeling anxious and wanted to intervene before this ugly disorder swallowed up his family for good. Tim felt certain that Beth was being deceitful, but he resolved to stay calm so as not to accuse his wife of something simply via conjecture.

Closing the car door, Tim opened his cell phone and tapped out a message: "Something came up and I can't make it tonight. I'll swing by your office tomorrow to pick up the folder. Sorry." Tim hit send and waited a beat for an answer. When a few minutes had passed without a reply, he started the car, put it in gear, and drove toward home and his family. He thought he might surprise the twins and start to assemble the Ping-Pong table once they went to bed.

What Tim hadn't seen was the sliver of light escaping from the parted curtains as Colleen Hughes snapped a photo of him getting out of his car which was clearly parked across the street from her home.

Chapter 36
Beth

As Beth's phone chirped that a text message had been received, she closed her eyes and massaged the bridge of her nose. A dull throbbing had lodged behind her eyes and was threatening to become a full-blown headache if she didn't get some Tylenol in her ASAP. This was the fourth new message she had received since leaving work at the retreat. GrannyQuilter007 needed to get a life. Sitting at the kitchen table, she tapped the screen of her Android to retrieve the latest communication and cocked her head when a photo appeared. *What the…? Why had…?*

Beth reverse pinched the screen to enlarge the photo. Tim was getting out of his car somewhere…but where? It looked like that expensive condo/townhome area that one of her recently widowed clients had moved into. Patricia had shown her endless pictures taken on her iPhone and carried on about how exclusive and wonderful the complex was until Beth had eventually tuned her out.

But why was Tim there?

The message read: "Beware HOARDER. I followed your husband here. I guess he found what you can't give him: A CLEAN and therefore happy home."

Beth folded her arms on the table and rested her throbbing head upon them. Up until now she had convinced herself that the messages from GrannyQuilter007 were some kind of a sick hoax, but this photo of Tim might prove otherwise. Maybe the secretive sender was actually one of her friends who didn't want to get in the middle of their problems. ...*Did they have problems?* Up until now she hadn't thought so. She felt confident in her marriage and was 100% sure that her husband was faithful. Had her hoarding, or rather her collecting, taken a toll on their relationship? Was she too blind or maybe too busy to see what was happening right beneath her nose?

"Mom, are you okay?"

Beth raised her head to Heather, who was wearing a jacket and carrying her purse. "Headache," Beth answered. "You going somewhere?"

"I'm heading over to Megan's. We're going to start studying for next week's midterms." Heather fished her keys from the bottom of her purse. "I'll be home by eleven thirty."

"What are the twins up to?"

"Joey is in bed playing a video game on Dad's tablet and Katy is talking on the phone. She just finished painting her nails."

"Do you know where Dad went?"

"He said he had an appointment to meet with a student who works during the day."

Nodding her head, Beth drew her lips in and gently bit down on them to stop from saying something she might later regret.

Heather paused a moment and Beth saw concern in her daughter's eyes.

"Are you sure you're okay, Mom? Can I get you a cup of tea or something?"

"No, honey, but thanks. I think I'm going to head straight to bed." Beth rose from the chair and felt somewhat unsteady. "And Heather, thanks for picking up dinner and staying around until I got home. You've been a big help."

"Sure, Mom. No problem."

Beth turned off all of the lights on the main floor, leaving a solitary bulb shining down on the range from the bottom of the microwave as a night-light for Heather and Tim. Scrawling a few words in block letters on a sticky note, she attached the yellow square to the television screen in the kitchen. This was their standard spot to leave messages. The whole family knew to check the front of the TV on the kitchen counter for updates.

WENT TO BED. BAD HEADACHE.

That should keep him at a distance. Beth did not want to see or talk to her husband, nor did she want to hear her cell phone happily chime that other messages from GrannyQuilter007 had arrived.

She needed time to think…to sort out what in the world was going on. Maybe she'd even talk to her friends. They'd all be together at the MQR tomorrow for the People-Behind-the-Retreat Dinner, but realistically there probably wouldn't be any time for a serious private conversation. She'd simply have to play it by ear and see how the evening unfolded.

Exhausted, with a throbbing head, and fearing her husband no longer loved her, Beth's extremely good day had turned ugly very fast as yet another text message sounded its arrival.

Chapter 37
Marge

"It seems as though I've been gone a week instead of a mere forty-eight hours," Marge told Phree and Sunnie as she entered the Bridge on Thursday morning. "It feels good to be back. I'm looking forward to returning to a routine with solid footing underneath me. It's been quite a ride these past few days."

"If you need to talk," Phree nodded toward her mother, "we're both here for you."

"You know," Marge smiled, "I think I'd like that. Or maybe more to the point, I think I *need* that."

"Would you like to have some breakfast first?" Sunnie asked.

"Thanks but I don't think I could handle any food at the moment. Howevvverrrr," she drew out the word, "maybe a gallon of coffee would pair nicely with this saga."

"I'll go get some carafes of coffee from the Mess Hall." Phree pushed aside some papers and stood to leave, then hesitated. "Are you sure you don't want to try some of Evelyn's blueberry coffee cake or maybe a homemade doughnut or two?"

"Oh my God, yes," Marge said. "Some of both please."

"You two catch up on retreat business while I'm gone." A moment after departing the office, Phree stuck her head back in the door demanding, "No discussion about Val until I get back."

Sunnie said, "We wouldn't think of it."

"So, catch me up on the retreat," Marge told Sunnie.

"I'm happy to say there've been no major glitches. Probably the most unexpected thing that happened was one of the toilets overflowed upstairs in the sleeping quarters. The poor woman was mortified. Maintenance had it taken care of immediately and housekeeping was standing by with a mop and disinfectant."

Sunnie continued with a brief account of all the nonevents over the past two days.

"For the most part, the women have all gotten along beautifully with the exception of a little political disagreement between some of the hand stitchers. They got a bit boisterous about, of all things, gun control, but within minutes they 'agreed to disagree' and went on to safer subjects."

"You'll especially like this—Heloise has been behaving like a dream and is making friends left and right." Stopping for a breath, Sunnie looked toward the ceiling as she thought for a moment. "The wool hand stitchers have decided to get together once a month for what they are calling a 'Wooly Bullie' meeting. Their motto is 'stitching with wool while shooting the bull.'"

"I love it," Marge said.

"The food's been incredible. Nedra has been diligent about updating all of the social media sites with photos and stories, and to top it off we booked seven more confirmations for the upcoming weeks."

Marge raised her eyebrows, nodded her head, and said, "Impressive."

"In addition, the Ship's Store is doing quite well." Sunnie removed a sheet of paper from the top of a stack and slid it toward Marge. "Here's the daily sales report with the grand total for the week reflected at the bottom."

Picking up the paper and glancing at it, Marge made a low whistle. "Holy moly."

"Helen has been very busy keeping the shelves stocked with quilting-related notions and fabrics. You know how it is…if someone has a cool new gadget everyone wants it whether they need it or not."

Marge nodded. She had firsthand experience with this phenomenon and most certainly knew how 'notion envy' spread like wildfire.

"Jelly Rolls and Charm Packs have been flying off the shelves, not to mention the good old standards like thread, sewing machine needles, and seam rippers. After a few more groups have gone through the retreat, we may need to reevaluate and increase the scope of what we're offering."

"Agreed," Marge said.

"All in all I'd say this whole week has been a huge success and everything ran like clockwork while you were gone." Sunnie nodded, grinned, and spread out her arms. "Our guests are all enthusiastically happy about the Mayflower Quilters Retreat."

The aroma of coffee preceded Phree's return to the Bridge by a few steps. "Here we go, ladies. Help yourselves. I got extra for Nedra—she should be here shortly and I was afraid the coffee cake would be gone by then."

Fresh blueberries glistened like sapphires in four generous pieces of coffee cake with a crown of buttery crumble topping each slice. Six plump doughnuts dressed in cinnamon, powdered sugar, and chocolate glaze rested on a plate of fine white china. MQR coffee mugs and two full carafes rounded out the still life of a perfect breakfast.

Lifting a carafe to pour coffee into the mugs, Marge said, "It's good to be home."

In the time it took the three women to consume the breakfast fare, Marge had recounted an abridged version of the 'Val Story' to her friends. It was Phree who needed the tissue box parked in front of her. Marge wondered if it was because Phree's daughter, Emily, was away at her first semester of college this fall and maybe the scenario hit a scary nerve for her friend—or maybe she was simply reminded how much she missed her only child.

"I hate to say it because you all know how much I like everything to be under control, but I think my family's going to be in a state of flux for a while. I have no idea where this latest drama is going to lead the Russell clan."

"You can count on us for anything you need," Phree said and Sunnie agreed by nodding.

"I've asked Val to join me for lunch at the retreat today. I'd like to take her on a tour and show her how all of our hard work has panned out. I thought it might give her a little time away from personal problems."

"I think that's a wonderful idea," Sunnie said. "Feel free to add my suite to the tour if you'd like."

"And the Crow's Nest, too," Phree added.

"Thanks," Marge said. "I'd like that very much,"

Feeling more centered than she had for the past two days, Marge focused on work. She had to admit that Sunnie had done a fabulous job of staying on top of matters. After about a half hour of catching up on communiques and a little bit of paper shuffling, she decided it was important to have her presence felt at the retreat. It was time to reconnect with the guests and staff. Her first stop would be the maintenance building.

Marge plucked a sweater from the peg by the door, as it was a bit of a hike to the largest outbuilding on the MQR campus. Nestled behind a thick stand of evergreens and completely hidden from the view of the main building, the maintenance department was about a four- to five-minute walk.

After the uncertainty and excitement of the past week, these few stolen moments felt like a vacation to Marge. The cool crispness of autumn felt refreshing as sunshine filtered through the nearly leafless trees, peppering the ground and fallen leaves with dots of brightness. Inhaling the damp, earthy scent of moldering vegetation, she slowed her typical fast pace to a stroll. Buzzing bees intent on feasting on fallen fruit ignored her as she passed by. Marge made a mental note to talk to Jim, the landscape architect, about possibly reestablishing the mini-orchard of apple, pear, and cherry trees. Perhaps a strategically placed beehive or two on the property could furnish the kitchen with honey and at the same time help maintain a healthy honey bee population.

The path leading to the maintenance building was about to turn past the screen of evergreens. Marge stopped, slid her ever-present notepad from her back pocket, and jotted down two words: orchard and beehives. As she stowed the small tablet back into her pocket the familiar motorized sound from one of several John Deere Gator utility vehicles approached from the direction of the maintenance building. The crew used these mini-vehicles to haul items and equipment from one end of the retreat to the other. Marge jokingly referred to these little workhorses as golf carts on steroids.

Steve, the maintenance foreman, pulled the Gator to the side of the path, allowing Marge to pass. The bed of the vehicle was filled with split wood that would be used in the main fireplace of the retreat. It would require many trips to fill the shed with firewood and then an ample amount would also be placed by the hearth for easy access. The nights had grown chilly, and the guests were enjoying the novelty and cozy comfort of a crackling fire in the evenings.

"Hey, Cap…can I help you with anything?" Steve asked.

Steven Bonini was a high-school classmate of her son, Zach, and had taken to calling her Cap rather than Mrs. Russell or Marge. In his final year at a local college, Steve was earning a degree in Industrial Building Engineering and Maintenance. When he applied for the job of foreman in the department, both Marge and Phree liked him instantly. "He's young, got a great attitude, and he's also learning the most current information there is to know about maintaining a complex of this size," Phree had said. "I say we snatch him up." And they did.

"I'd like to get your feedback on this first week and see if you or your crew might have any thoughts or suggestions."

Steve leaned back and rested his right arm across the back of the passenger seat. "We're all happy at how smoothly everything went. So far this week the only emergency has been a stuffed up toilet in one of the guest rooms and a burned out bulb high in the foyer that we pulled the cherry picker in to change. Other than that everything has gone smoothly and run on schedule."

A few minutes of polite small talk followed and Marge thanked Steve for the excellent job he was doing. "I'm happy you joined us at the MQR, Steve, and we certainly hope you plan to stay with us after graduation."

"To be honest, Cap…I love it here. Not only do I enjoy the atmosphere of the retreat but I'm able to be close to my parents and help them."

Marge recalled from the interview with this young man that he was an only child and his father had recently had a heart attack. "How's your dad doing?"

"He's been back to work for a month now. It was only half days to start with but this past week he bumped it up to full time. He's tired when he gets home at night but he seems to be happy and doing quite well."

"I'm glad to hear it. Please tell both your parents I said hello."

Steve put the Gator in gear. "Will do," he said and patted the seat next to him. "Wanna lift?"

Smiling, Marge answered, "Thanks, but I rather like the walk in this weather."

By the time Val was due to arrive at the MQR, Marge had visited every department at the retreat and spoken with each person in charge. She made it a point to thank them all for their hard work of the past week and their attention to every detail. She had also spent time with the passengers, discussing their quilty projects and enjoying their stories. When Marge approached Heloise she was greeted with a smile.

"I've missed seeing you here these past few days," H said. "There's something I'd like to say to you in private."

Marge was sure she was in for a verbal beatdown after the way she had spoken to this woman on Sunday and Monday. Heloise had most likely been doing a slow burn over the exchange and Marge was surely going to hear about it. Thank goodness H had the sense to keep it private and not make a scene in front of all the other guests. "Shall we meet in my office in say…fifteen minutes?" Val was due for her tour in half an hour and Marge prayed her daughter would not be early for the first time in her life.

"That will suit me." Heloise lowered her head and returned her focus to the block she was piecing.

Marge began mentally preparing a humble and sincere apology as she moved on to chat with the next guest.

"Come in," Marge smiled as she stood and walked around her desk to escort one of their first and most infamous guests to a seat. "What can I help you with today?" Marge closed the door hoping to signal to anyone approaching the Bridge that she wanted privacy.

Heloise waited for Marge to sit at her desk before speaking. "You can help by accepting my apology. Or should I say apologies," the woman answered. "I'm sorry I was such a…such a bad-tempered excuse of a quilter on check-in."

Marge waved off her comment. "Nonsense. No need to apologize."

"I'm afraid there is. I wasn't a very nice person and poor Shirley and you got the brunt of my rudeness."

"It's water under the bridge and truth be told I'd like to apologize to you for my snarky comments the day of the L-R-C game. It wasn't very hospitable of me and certainly not very professional."

"I got what I deserved." Heloise paused. "I don't know why I act that way. I feel I have to put up a wall so no one can get close to me. I have no good reason for what I do, but after this week I'm going to try my best *not* to continue doing it."

"It's been fun watching you grow into quite the celebrity around here." Marge smiled.

"No one is more surprised than me," Heloise beamed, "and I find myself enjoying the friendships that I always so blithely scoffed at. Shirley and I have been discussing coming back as roommates next spring."

Marge grabbed at her chest and mocked a heart attack. "Will miracles never cease?"

Laughing, Heloise stood, offering her hand to Marge. "It's been my pleasure, Marge Russell, GM and Captain of the Mayflower Quilters Retreat." The two women shook hands and H added, "You sure do run a tight ship around here, young lady."

Chapter 38
Dr. Colleen Hughes

Every time Colleen heard footfalls or male voices in the reception area outside of her office, the pounding in her chest increased to the point where she feared she might have a heart attack. After all the precautions she had taken by using cash to purchase a cheap cell phone with airtime so she could send untraceable e-mails and texts to Beth, she had gotten impatient and slipped up last night. Sending Beth a photo of Tim and his car in front of her house had been thrilling but unwise. Even if his wife didn't know where the photo was taken, Tim certainly would.

What in the world was I thinking?

The truth was that Colleen had been angry when she received Tim's text that something had come up and he couldn't make it. What did he mean he couldn't make it? He had been sitting in front of her townhouse for over ten minutes! Without thinking, she snapped a photo and sent it through cyberspace as proof of Tim Stevenson's alleged infidelity and, unfortunately, her own stupidity.

She would deny it. If he confronted her with the electronic communiques, she could say that GrannyQuilter007 must have followed him and was playing a nasty trick. She was innocent of the charges and had no idea who might be behind such shameful behavior. That would work—it would *have* to work. Other than that damn picture, there was no way to track any of this back to her.

Was it so wrong to be attracted to a colleague, someone who was her equal? He was clearly unhappy with his life. Who in their right mind would want to be saddled with a hoarder for God's sake? She knew she could make him happy and she was young enough that maybe they could even have a…

Hearing a man's voice, she then heard the receptionist say, "Please have a seat, Professor Stevenson. I'll tell her you're here."

After identifying Tim's voice, her heart missed several beats—and not in a good way. Colleen was convinced that soon she'd be on her way to the hospital via an ambulance.

Deny, deny, deny!

Tim entered the room. Expecting to see him upset and angry, she was shocked by his demeanor.

"Is this a bad time?" he asked with his trademark sexy smile.

Oh wow, how fantastic he looked!

"Not at all, Tim. Have a seat." She noticed he closed the door behind him this time. If she could pull this off, it would be quite a coup and worth every nerve-wracking second. *His foolish wife either hasn't confronted him or he shares my desires. What an idiot Beth Stevenson is!*

At the same time they both said, "I'm sorry…" and then they each chuckled.

Tipping his head and extending his hand, Tim said, "Ladies first."

"Why, thank you, kind sir." Was that admiration she saw in his eyes? "I want to apologize for forgetting the packet of information I had prepared for you yesterday. There's no excuse, except that I was in a hurry to leave the house in the morning and simply left it behind."

Tim waved her off. "No harm, no foul."

A brilliant scenario occurred to Colleen out of nowhere and she ran with it. "It's probably just as well that you couldn't make it last night. I wasn't home but I told my roommate to give you the envelope. Naturally it was sealed so she wouldn't have had any idea what it contained." Of course there was no roommate, but if she claimed not to be home...well then, she could *not* have been the one who sent the photo to his wife. "This will work out better anyway. We can take some time to go over the material together."

"I appreciate that," Tim said.

Coyly, Colleen asked, "And you are sorry for what exactly?"

Tim looked bewildered for a moment. "Oh...oh, that...yes. I was going to tell you that I was sorry that I was unable to meet you last night. Although it seems as though it might have been for the best if you weren't even home."

"Tell me how Beth is doing, poor thing. It must be difficult for you being stuck in an unhappy marriage. Surely you would thrive with a more equal or...shall I say educated woman."

Tim narrowed his eyes. "Colleen, I'm not in an unhappy marriage and my wife is one of the most intelligent women I know. If you remember correctly, I never told you that I was unhappy. I apologize if somehow you got the wrong impression."

She watched Tim stiffen and then look at his watch. "I must apologize yet again. I'm afraid I'm short on time. I have a meeting in less than ten minutes and I need to get going. I'll be fine going over the information by myself—no use taking up any more of your time than I already have. Thank you for all of your help. If I have any questions is it okay if I contact you?"

Colleen felt as though she had been sucker-punched by this guy as heat rose to her cheeks. On the other hand, he honestly could have an appointment that he needed to get to. Surely he'd rather spend time with her if at all possible. "Maybe over lunch or dinner?" she asked.

Tim rose from the chair. "I'm sorry but that won't work for me and I really want to get in touch with your contact as soon as possible." Tim smiled and reached out his hand for the envelope.

Colleen clutched the information tight to her chest.

Keeping his arm extended and his hand open he added, "Once again I really appreciate all that you have done to help my family and me."

They were at a standoff and neither moved.

"Colleen, is there a problem here? May I please have the information? As I said, I really need to get to a meeting across campus."

Could it be that he preferred...maybe even loved his hoarding quilting wife? *Screw him! Screw both of them!* She felt tears forming but rather than suffer further embarrassment by appearing to be an infatuated fool, she thrust the envelope at him and said, "Best of luck to both of you. I hope you can find a way to overcome your wife's unfortunate condition."

Chapter 39
Beth

Even though Beth's headache was long gone, when Tim placed a hand on her shoulder this morning and asked how she was feeling she fake mumbled, "Not too good."

"I'll get Katy and Joey off to school. Stay in bed and try to shake this thing."

He brushed aside her hair, bent over, kissed her temple, and left their bedroom.

Laying there listening to the morning squabbles while waiting for everyone to clear out, Beth's emotions swung between anger, disbelief, revenge, and sadness. How was she ever going to get through this day until she could talk with her friends this evening at the retreat? When she heard the garage door rumble up and then go back down right away, she knew her husband had left for work.

More tubs needed to get to the storage shed today. When that chore was finished, she could breathe easily again...except for the fact that Beth sensed something was going on behind her back. Something was adrift and about to change. There had been a shift. She could feel it. The little hairs at the back of her neck stood up like an electrical storm had passed through her body.

Leaning against the kitchen counter, Beth nestled a mug of coffee in both of her hands. She had no appetite for food this morning and instead borrowed some time to watch the backyard birds swoop between the feeder and the birdbath. The cliché 'free as a bird' came to her and she longed for freedom from what shackled her. Sickened by a power which she was unable to control, Beth sunk to her knees in a puddle of grief and sobbed.

A monster had sneaked into her life, taken control, and slowly stolen her ability to make suitable choices about her possessions. Little by little her peace of mind had been chipped away, and Beth was left feeling isolated, lonely, and sad. Worst of all, she had deceived her husband in order to protect her inner demons. She did *not* like the woman she had become. Seriously, who could blame Tim or the kids if they were fed up with her?

Somebody help me…please!

She needed to change and today was the day.

Feeling hopeful, Beth pulled herself up from the floor. Drying her eyes and clearing her nose with a tissue, she made a solemn vow that she would beat this thing. She would need a fresh start and a clean slate to succeed…wouldn't she? At the very least she deserved that.

I'll make a quick run with an empty tub and do one last 'power sweep' throughout the house. I don't have time today to pick through a bunch of stuff and decide what needs to be tossed and what should be saved or donated or recycled. I simply need to get those final bins out of the basement and over to the storage shed…and then *I'll change.*

Optimism radiated from Beth as she made her way down the basement stairs. Their lives would return to normal, Tim and the kids would still love her, and everything would be safely stored away.

She might be on the verge of losing her husband, but she'd be damned if she would lose her treasures, too.

Chapter 40
Tim

That was weird!

The woman could *not* have been more obvious unless she had a flashing neon light over her head that read: "I'm flirting with you!"

What part of 'I'm married' doesn't she understand?

I guess I won't be asking her for help again anytime soon.

Tim headed off to his office and his 'fake' meeting.

Chapter 41
Val

"I saved the best for last," Marge said. "This is where the fun and magic happens. We call it the Hannah Brewster Quilting Room."

It was hard for Val to believe that earlier today she had been dreading this visit to the MQR that her mother had suggested. Mom had been so excited about showing off the retreat, not to mention how helpful and patient she'd been over the past few days, that Val had put on a happy face and agreed to a tour. Now, she wished it didn't have to end!

She had never understood her mother's obsession with quilting. Val was aware how much Mom enjoyed being with her quilting friends and what a great support group they were for each other but...holy cow, all that sewing and cutting and work was way beyond her scope of what she would consider 'fun.' But this big, beautiful building full of happy—really happy—people all chatting and sharing something they loved had not only taken her mind away from her problems, but actually made her rather envious.

Sure, most of the women at the retreat were way older than she was. Heck, a lot of them were even older than Mom, but there were a few younger quilters too. Val watched three girls who had to be in their twenties sitting side by side with sewing machines whirring. One girl bent over her machine and said something—the other two stopped sewing and leaned in to listen. They all began laughing so hard that one of the girls grabbed at her crotch and bolted from the room causing the other two to laugh even harder—Val found herself laughing too.

Mom introduced her to most of the quilters and told everyone that her daughter was home from college for a visit. Even though she was unable to keep track of all of the names, when Mom introduced Heloise, Val remembered the story Mom told about someone the staff had nicknamed H.

"How nice to be able to get home for a few days," Heloise said after stopping her sewing machine.

Val could have placed a bet on what the next question would be. Every single woman had asked her the same thing, and she had answered politely by smiling and telling each of them that she wasn't into quilting.

"Are you a quilter, dear?"

There it was.

Expecting to repeat her standard answer, Val was surprised when she heard herself say, "Not yet, but I'm hoping Mom can start teaching me some of the basics soon."

Marge had been keeping a sharp watch on the goings-on in the room, but Val noticed her attention snap back to the conversation.

"That'll be fun for both of you…what a treat," Heloise said. "Who knows, maybe someday you'll even follow in your mother's footsteps and work at this fabulous retreat."

"I think that would be amazing," Val answered. "What do you think, Mom?"

Marge was the epitome of dumbstruck—slack mouthed, glazed eyes, and utterly speechless.

Val laughed and in a loud whisper said to Heloise, "I think we've just shocked her."

On the way back to the Bridge, Marge pulled Val close. "You were just toying with me back there, weren't you?"

Acting innocent, Val said, "What do you mean?"

"You know what I mean…all that 'I want Mom to teach me how to quilt and work here when I grow up' stuff."

"Actually, I'm not kidding. This looks like a blast and I've always loved your quilts. Do you think I could learn?"

"Of course you could learn and I'd love to teach you!" Marge stopped walking and rested her hands on her cheeks in sheer joy.

"Does it take long to learn?"

"To be honest, you never finish learning how to make quilts. You just keep working and experimenting and growing. I think that's a lot of the appeal…it never gets old."

"I think I'd like to learn, but right now I obviously don't have much money for stuff."

Putting an arm around her daughter, Marge said, "Honey, I have enough fabric in my stash, not to mention two extra sewing machines, that neither of us would have to buy anything for the next twenty years."

Chapter 42
Beth

The Meet the People-Behind-the-Retreat Dinner had been a huge success for both the staff and the guests. During dessert Marge had made a short speech and then introduced the board members. There was a short question-and-answer period where all the remarks had been positive with a lot of joking and laughter filling the Quilters Mess Hall.

Prior to dining, Marge had privately asked the board members to reconvene in the conference room for a few minutes after dinner. "I'll keep it short," she had said.

Secretly pleased, Beth thought this would give her the opportunity she had hoped for with all of her friends together. But now that it was close to happening, she found herself reluctant to share what had been going on in her life. Did she really want to tell everyone that Tim was possibly cheating on her? That someone had been stalking her about hoarding? That she had rented a storage locker to deceive her husband? Maybe she needed to rethink her approach. After all, none of these things sounded very pretty.

"No gavel tonight." Marge stood at the head of the table. "This isn't an official board meeting. On behalf of Phree, Sunnie, and myself we'd like to thank you for everything you've done to make our soft opening and first week of the Mayflower Quilters Retreat a success."

The women applauded softly.

"Moving forward we plan to iron out any wrinkles that have arisen..."

Rosa interrupted and asked, "Will that be dry heat or

with steam?"

The women laughed.

"Thank you for that quilty reference to ironing, Rosa," Marge said.

"Always my pleasure."

"As nice as it was for all of us to be here for dinner with our guests this evening, we won't be doing this every week. It's too much to ask of everyone, especially since most of our sewing and quilting time has been cut short these past few weeks by extracurricular retreat activities. Nedra goes back to her 'real' job next week," Marge made air quotes, "and I can tell you that we will miss her around here terribly. She's done a great job with the retreat's presence on social media."

Nedra nodded. "I can't tell you how much I've enjoyed being here. It's going to be difficult to wrap my head around traveling to the city again every day."

Marge sat down. "The Ship's Store has been extremely successful and Helen has stayed busy keeping items in stock. The Pampered Pilgrim received high praise both for Beth's wonderful work and also for our masseuse, Tori."

Beth was pleased with the acknowledgement. She had promised Andrea that she would come by the retreat on check-out day to style her hair again before her 'almost-ex' dropped off their daughter.

Checking her notes Marge continued. "Lettie's spinning classes are completely full for next week. Since she only has five spinning wheels she'll be busy repeating classes—the excitement is off the charts from the correspondence I've been receiving. We'll have Rosa's Quilts of Valor theme running over the week of Veterans Day...which really isn't that far off. And last but not least, we are almost through working out the details for Nancy's two-day mystery quilt workshop that will be offered once a month during random weeks."

"So, ladies, that about sums it up. Our passengers will

disembark tomorrow afternoon by three when we will reset everything for a new group to come in on Sunday."

Beth watched Marge set her notes down slowly and then look at each of the women. "One final thought I'd like to share...this retreat, which we have *all* worked so hard to build up, is one heck of a great place to work every day. I am honored to be a part of it." She spread her arms wide and smiled broadly. "It just doesn't get any better than this."

During the light applause, Beth knew there would be no time tonight in which to discuss her woes. It was late and everyone wanted to get out of here and head home. The more she thought of it, the more comfortable she was *not* sharing her business quite yet.

The bad news was that she would be heading home, where she would face her husband for the first time since receiving a photo of him allegedly in front of some woman's house yesterday.

Tim stood before the sink wearing an apron and placing two dinner plates in the drying rack. "What's going on?" she asked as she came through the back door.

"Oh, hey there, honey. Just cleaning up after dinner."

She watched him nest three plastic deli containers and drop an empty glass jelly jar inside of them. Tim gently bent the plastic lids and pushed them inside of the containers. Her mouth went dry as he opened the cabinet door beneath the sink and tossed the whole thing into the recycle bin. She *never* got rid of plastic containers and especially a perfectly good glass jar—there were too many potential uses for these perfectly good reusable items and once nested the plastic containers barely took up any space. It felt as though there was a vise on her heart, squeezing it abnormally, causing irregular beats.

Stay calm. You can rescue them when he's not around. She was reminded of her vow: today was supposed to be her 'new beginning.' *It's better if I start tomorrow. After all it really doesn't make sense to shift gears in the middle of a day.*

Tim sounded a little annoyed. "So what do you think?"

"Huh?" She hadn't heard a word he had said.

"My idea—what do you think of my idea?"

"Um...sorry, I was thinking about what was going on at the retreat tonight and missed what you said."

Tim had removed the apron and draped it over a kitchen chair. It wasn't until he set two mugs next to the tea cozy that she noticed he had made a pot of tea. "The twins are asleep and Heather is studying in her room. Let's go into the family room where we can be comfortable." He held out his hand with the empty mugs and, with a nod, motioned for her to lead the way. When Beth stepped in front of him he said, "We need to talk."

Bile rose in her throat and the vise around her heart squeezed tighter. "About what?" she asked. *Your girlfriend? The storage shed? My alleged hoarding?*

Tim didn't answer her question but said, "Let's sit on the couch."

She plopped on the cushion and crossed her arms like a pouty child. She was not going to make this easy for him. Thoughts swirled in Beth's anguished mind. *Side by side on the sofa...how cozy. What a great way to tell your wife you've been cheating on her!* "What's this all about, Tim?"

She could tell that her husband felt uncomfortable. His hand shook slightly when he handed her a mug of Earl Grey. Beth took the proffered beverage from him and immediately set it on the coffee table. "Can we please get to the point?"

Running a hand slowly through his hair, Tim exhaled and said, "This is very difficult, Beth, and there's no easy way to tell you."

He tried to pry one of her hands away from her biceps but she pulled away from him. Beth could feel the sting of tears beginning but clenched her teeth to stem their flow. *You two-timing son of a ...*

"I want you to know that I love you. I've loved you from the moment I sat in your chair for a haircut all those years ago and we talked about history. I love you, I love our kids, I love our life together..."

Droplets fell freely over Beth's cheeks and she noticed that Tim was struggling with tears of his own. She wouldn't soften. He would have to be man enough to admit what he had done.

"I want to help you. I don't want to lose you. I think we can tackle this together and make it work."

Now Beth was utterly confused. *What the heck is he talking about?*

"I've been doing some research about hoarding."

"I'M NOT A HOARDER," she shouted so fast that it surprised her. "I'm sick of everyone thinking I'm a hoarder." She started to stand. "I've had enough."

"Okay, okay," he said and held up his hands. "We have to stay calm. Can we talk about this before it gets completely out of control?"

"What do you mean 'out of control'...look around you," Beth was angry and swept her arm to take in the family room. "Where's the mess? If I was a hoarder this place would be full of junk and crap and mold. I'd say our home is relatively clean for a family of five." She was sounding shrill and hated what she was doing but she continued anyway. If she made it awkward enough, he might stop. "I do have a job you know and I'm not the only one in this house with a license to operate the vacuum or the washer and dryer!"

Exasperated, Tim's shoulders slumped. "Beth, I only want to talk. Can we simply have a calm dialogue? Please?"

"Go ahead. Say what you have to say. But I have a few things of my own I'd like to clear up when you're finished."

Tim pulled his lower lip between his teeth and rolled his eyes to the ceiling. After a deep breath he said, "I want us to see someone."

"What do you mean? Someone like who?"

"As I said, I've done some research and I have the name of a respected therapist. I think you're..."

Beth interrupted. "A therapist is going to make me throw everything away. You might as well save your money because I won't do it. The house is clean and livable. Why does what I do matter so damn much to everyone else if it makes me happy?"

"I *know* you're hoarding things, Beth. If we don't address what's going on, it's going to get worse. We need to stay on top of the issue before it swallows us up. I really don't want to argue about this. And I desperately don't want to lose you to a pile of useless junk."

Thunderstruck, Beth tried one final tactic. "Again..." Once more she flung her arm out indicating the room. "Where's all this so-called hoarded junk you refer to?"

"That's exactly what I'd like to know," Tim answered.

"What's *that* supposed to mean?"

"Oh, Beth." Tim gentled his voice trying to be patient, yet it was obvious that he was saddened. "We both know you've been removing things from the house all week...ever since there was talk of getting a Ping-Pong table for the basement. I have no idea where you're putting all the stuff that was down there. I'm not blind nor am I stupid, but some sort of exodus has been going on around here."

It was clear she had been found out.

"And to tell you the truth," Tim continued, "I don't know what's worse—the fact that you've been deceiving me or the fact that you thought you had no choice but to deceive me."

"I'm not getting rid of anything if that's what this is all about. I've really got this whole thing under control." Sobs took over her tears and represented her shame. Beth's tough persona cracked and crumbled after feeling the comfort of Tim's support when he slipped his arm around her shoulders. "I...It's...I can't stop. I can't do it. I want to stop, but I just can't. It freezes me. I'm helpless unless I give in."

"Shhh," he breathed into her hair. "It's going to be okay, honey. I love you no matter what."

After several minutes had passed, in a much calmer voice, Beth whispered, "I want to hear your ideas, but not until you answer some of my questions first."

Chapter 43
Marge

The house was quiet when Marge arrived home. She assumed Val must be in bed or maybe had fallen asleep on the couch. Several moments passed as Marge stood over the stack from today's mail making two piles: one for bills and one for the garbage.

Val entered the kitchen in her pajamas. "I know you're probably tired, Mom, but can we talk for a few minutes? It won't take long." Her daughter pulled a red-and-white vinyl chair away from the '50s style retro table and sat down.

"Of course, honey," she smiled and sat across from Val. "It always takes time to unwind after work no matter how tired I am, especially when I get home late." Marge had passed tired over three hours ago and was currently approaching dead tired, but when your troubled kid wants to talk...you oblige. "What's up?"

"I've been thinking...you know, about what I should do."

Marge nodded.

"Anyway, I have an idea or maybe just part of an idea but I think it's a start. I know what I want, I just don't know how I can achieve it."

"Okay."

"Oh, Mom, I don't know...maybe the whole thing's stupid after all."

"Go ahead. We'll figure it out."

"Well, a lot of this will fall on you and Dad and if you don't want to be involved..."

Marge snorted as she said, "For God's sake Val, would you just spit it out!"

"The first thing is that I've decided I'd like to keep the baby. The next thing is that I want to get some kind of an education so someday I can support the two of us."

Marge thought she had never been prouder of her daughter than at this moment. Not risking the emotion in her voice, she nodded.

"I guess it's pretty obvious that I…we…will need to live here for a while."

"You are both welcome for as long as it takes."

"Thanks, Mom. I hoped you'd say that. Now this is where it gets a little sketchy and maybe even sounds a little weird. When I was at the retreat today…it's hard to explain but everyone was so nice, both the quilters and the staff. Everybody seemed so happy to be there the atmosphere reminded me a little of when you took Zach and me to Disneyworld when were little."

Chuckling, Marge said, "That's a good analogy."

"I meant it when I said I wanted you to teach me how to quilt. It looked like the whole retreat was friends and having fun. Something clicked for me and I wanted to stay there. It felt safe. I started to wonder if I might be able to work there part time while I go to school. I know it sounds crazy but I could do any type of work. Maybe I could work in housekeeping or the dining room or even do landscaping or maintenance." Val looked down at the table and said in a low voice, "Tell me if you think this is stupid."

"Nothing you have said is stupid, Val. It sounds to me like you've put a lot of thought into the situation and come up with some good ideas."

"I Googled classes at Sauk Trail Community and wrote down some possibilities." She reached behind her and pulled an index card off the counter. "If I went full time, in two years I'd have an associate degree. It'll probably take longer than two years with a baby and working, but at some point I'd have a degree. There are also some courses where I could get certificates and they don't take as long as an associate."

"I'm impressed with your research."

"I guess it's time that I accept what I did and stop thinking it's going to go away someday. But right now, I still wish it hadn't happened."

"I understand perfectly."

"Is that bad? It doesn't mean I won't love the baby does it? It just means that I wish I hadn't messed up. Did you...did you feel that way about Jacob?"

"You bet I did. I think it's normal under the circumstances but once you see that little boy or girl you'll never want your life any other way."

"I'm just sorry for you and Dad. I know this isn't what you wanted for me. I've made a pretty big mess."

"Oh...we'll survive. And so will you, sweetie."

"As long as we're on the subject, there's one more thing I'd like to talk about."

"What's that?"

"I want to tell you who the father is."

Chapter 44
Tim

"What! What do you mean am I seeing another woman?"

"Well are you?"

"Of course I'm not. What the hell gave you that idea?" Tim shot out of his seat and walked to the center of the room while both of his hands combed through his hair. He exhaled heavily and his hands flopped to his thighs.

"Someone has been…well, the only way I can put it is someone has been stalking me."

"What? Tim shouted. And you didn't think I needed to know this?"

"I was embarrassed."

"Beth, that doesn't make any sense."

"Well, it kind of does." Beth reached for her cell phone. "I've been getting e-mails and texts since Tuesday from someone who goes by GrannyQuilter007. They start here." She slid the phone toward him.

He looked at the screen showing the single word HOARDER! "This is awful! God, Beth, who's this GrannyQuilter person?"

"I can't even guess. I've been trying to figure it out for days." Pointing at the phone Beth said, "Keep scrolling."

Tim kept reading and scrolling.

"…your children will hate you." Scroll.

"Your husband will leave you." Scroll.

"How many of these are there?" he asked.

"A lot," Beth answered.

"The exodus has already started…" Scroll.

"This is horrible! I still don't understand why you didn't tell me."

"It was embarrassing and I was ashamed. Keep going."

Tim kept scrolling through e-mail after e-mail.

"A wandering eye! Bullshit! This is really pissing me off."

When Tim reached the final e-mail, he set the phone on the coffee table. "And you have no idea? None at all?"

Beth picked up her Android, tapped several commands, and handed the phone back to her husband. "These are the texts. There's only a few of them."

It took less than thirty seconds for Tim to reach the photo of him at Colleen's townhouse. He slammed his fist on the coffee table. "That bitch!"

Beth winced. "So there *is* another woman."

"Yeah, but definitely not like you think."

His wife was crying again. She had her face covered with both of her hands in shame. "I can't believe you told someone that I'm a hoarder!"

He tried to pry one of her hands from her face but again she pulled away from him.

"I'm so humiliated."

"She's a psychologist, Beth. I was desperate. She's helped us before." None of these reasons seemed to help the situation. Tim placed a hand over his mouth, clutched his fingers together and then dragged his hand down toward his chin. "I had no idea she would hurt you like this."

"Hurt me! She was trying to ruin our marriage and steal you for herself!"

"I'm going to report her for unethical behavior tomorrow morn…"

"NO!" Beth slapped her hands on her knees and glared at him. She was seething. "Don't. You. Dare," she spat out. "That's all I need is a million more people knowing that my husband thinks I'm a hoarder."

" But…"

"NO! I mean it, Tim."

"Don't you think she should be called out for this?"

"Not at my expense. It would be so humiliating." Beth was down to sniffling now and she grabbed Tim's arm. "Please don't. I'm begging you."

Tim paced the family room floor. He wanted to punch something. The thought of Colleen Hughes doing this to someone else when he could prevent it made him feel sick. How many people had she already crossed the line with by means of unscrupulous behavior?

"Promise me," Beth whispered.

He had decided that without Beth's knowledge he would make one more private visit to the not-so-good doctor first thing in the morning and blast her with a stern ultimatum. The only reason that she was not getting her butt hauled before the appropriate authorities was because he didn't want to see his wife humiliated any further. He would keep records of all the e-mails and texts she had sent to Beth and he would also be getting advice from his lawyer on the subject. He'd end his tirade by telling her, "If I catch wind that you've hurt anyone else by being unethical, I'll pull the plug on you."

Beth repeated her words, "Please Tim, promise me."

It took a moment to form the words so he wouldn't actually be lying *and* so he could take advantage of an opportunity. "I promise you that I will not report Dr. Hughes for her behavior in this matter and that I will not do anything that will further embarrass you. But," Tim paused.

Beth narrowed her eyes. "But what?"

"You have to agree that we'll go to a therapist together."

Chapter 45
Marge

Life was good in Marge's world as she drove to work on Friday morning. Nothing could possibly spoil this wonderful day. The sun was shining and the day promised to be warm and balmy.

This was checkout day at the MQR and as far as she could tell, the soft opening had been triumphant. All the guests would be gone by three o'clock this afternoon and the staff would be in full swing resetting everything for the new passengers to check in at noon on Sunday.

Val was moving forward by making good decisions about her future. Marge found she was especially thrilled that on her next day off work she would begin the tradition of passing her quilting knowledge on to her daughter.

Halfway to the retreat Marge's phone rang. The moment she heard the voice at the other end she froze. There *was* something that could spoil the day after all: her irrational sister, Laura.

"Well, it's good to know you're still alive."

"Yep, I'm still kicking," Marge said attempting to be jovial but wishing she hadn't answered the phone.

"Considering you haven't had the courtesy to get back to me, I thought you might have died and no one bothered to let me know."

Marge sighed. *Here we go.* But Marge wouldn't take the bait. "Nope. I'm fine.

"So what's your excuse for ignoring me? And don't give me that same old story that you're busy with your kids.

They're old enough to take care of themselves by now."

Well, thank you, Dr. Laura Spock for your brilliant insight on child rearing. "Actually, I have been busy helping Val with something. Not to mention our first week with guests at the retreat." *Keep it light – don't let her get to you.*

"I saw that retreat thing splashed all over the media. You'd think it was a big deal or something."

"For some people it is."

Laura scoffed. "Like people with no life."

Marge pressed down on her lips and then made a raspberry sound. "Look, I'm pulling into work. We'll have to do this another time." *Over my dead body.*

"Just answer me this…what the hell has been so important that you can't take a few minutes to contact your sister once in a while?"

Without thinking Marge blurted, "Val is pregnant and we've moved her back home." Assuming that any rational thinking person would accept this as a valid reason to be tied up for a few days, Marge expected a comment along the lines of, 'Oh my goodness, poor girl. Keep me posted and if there's anything I can do for either of you…'

But instead, Laura snorted. "I always knew that girl was going to be a trouble. Like mother like daughter I guess."

The blood in Marge's loving mother's heart ran cold. She pushed the button on her phone and disconnected the call.

I won't take part anymore in your nasty comments and hateful arguments…even if you are my sister.

From now on, Laura…I'm through with you.

Chapter 46
Beth

"Okay, that's fair. I'll agree to go to a therapist with you as long as the two of you don't gang up on me and force me to do things I'm not comfortable doing."

"Agreed," Tim said.

Beth was emotionally drained but she was also curious and a bit apprehensive about what her husband had in mind.

"I want you to know that I respect how difficult this is for you. I have some ideas, and they may not all be good ones, but hear me out. We've already agreed that both of us will see a therapist and I feel that's our number one step to take."

Beth nodded. "Okay."

"I know you've been storing bins somewhere but I'm not sure where. I'm guessing you've recently rented a storage locker or something. What if we tried this idea...what if we got the biggest storage shed the village allows for our backyard."

Beth folded her arms.

"Relax, honey. Don't go putting up that folded-arm wall again. We're going to figure this out. Let's say we can have a ten-foot by twelve-foot shed. That's pretty darn big."

Beth kept a poker face as she determined the size shed he was talking about was *way* bigger than her little four by eight storage locker *and* with the added convenience that it would be in her own yard.

"We could install racks or shelving units or whatever you need. You could store anything you want in there. It would be all your space with no prying eyes or no judgments made."

"What's the catch?"

"That everything stays in the shed. You don't fill it up and then start filtering boxes and bins back into the house or garage. The house is for us, for our family, to have a peaceful and clean space. The shed is yours to do whatever you please."

While it sounded like a good solution, Beth felt clammy as she already worried what she would do when the shed was full. But Tim must have been able to read her mind. He took her hands in his.

"I'm sure you're probably wondering what will happen when there's no more room in the shed. I'm sorry to say this but from my research it sounds as though there is no cure for hoarding. Sorry, I know you hate that word. *But* there are many behavioral strategies we'll both be learning from the therapist and together I'm confident that we *will* conquer the most difficult aspects. I'm counting on the fact that by the time the shed is full, we'll have a grasp on how to better control your anxiety."

"Do you really think it's possible?"

"I do, Beth." He drew her into an embrace and kissed her forehead. "I've always known that together we can do anything."

"Then I'm all in."

Chapter 47
Marge

No one talks about my child that way. No one! Heat rose in Marge's face as she clenched her teeth in anger. *I have to let go of this nonsense with my sister once and for all. There's no reason to be around people who make me feel bad. As the saying goes...life is too short.*

The contented introspection which Marge had enjoyed before Laura phoned had been replaced by the bitter taste of disappointment. Struggling to overcome the angst which had intruded on her well-being was like an unexpected spring tornado raging on a peaceful day. That's exactly what Laura's negative personality was like—a tornado...spinning, dark, angry and demanding, swooping down and altering an otherwise calm moment in the lives she touched.

And just like in the aftermath of a tornado, Marge needed to pick up the pieces and move forward. Today promised to be a busy day at the retreat as the guests departed for home. She needed to stay on point, not be overwhelmed by her sister's meanness. This time she had gone too far.

"Buh-bye, Laura," Marge said out loud. "In order to have peace in my heart I forgive you— but I will not be a slave to your cruelness any longer. I wish you a nice life."

On the short walk from the parking lot to the retreat building Marge passed several women already schlepping items to their vehicles. "Morning Marge," Marie called out. "Just getting my bedroom stuff out to the car so I can keep sewing till the last minute."

"Great idea," Marge replied.

Down the length of the porch rested piles of luggage, tote bags, sewing machine cases, and all forms of traveling gear awaiting the arrival of Ricky Mitchell shortly after one o'clock. *His tip jar is going to be overflowing,* Marge thought with a smile.

Upon entering through the doors of the retreat, she noticed a definite shift in the atmosphere from the previous several days. As usual, there was still a lot of hustling activity, but it was geared more to packing and leaving than sewing and chatting. A few guests who had farther to travel or simply desired to get home earlier in the day were already close to leaving. Nedra was capturing images of the mass exodus on her cameras and Marge was certain that a wrap-up blog post would hit cyberspace later this afternoon.

The Bridge was empty, which didn't surprised Marge as Sunnie and Phree were most likely mingling or helping the passengers. She hoped to steal a few moments to check new e-mails and phone messages before the day got too far away from her. It wasn't long before Marge had tuned out the surrounding activity and was attending to upcoming retreat business. The weeks and months ahead were filling up nicely with reservations.

Sunnie entered the office accompanied by a loud, "Whew. It's crazy out there." She dropped into her office chair. "I don't think anyone wants to leave here."

"Fill me in."

"A couple of things," began Sunnie. "Most people want some kind of a contact information swap. This time I just passed a piece of lined paper around the room and announced if they want to be part of the info sharing to fill out whatever they are comfortable with…such as e-mail, street address, phone number, etcetera. We'll make copies for anyone participating and hand them out before they leave. We need to come up with some kind of pre-printed form to pass around. I'll noodle it through before the end of next week gets here."

Nodding, Marge said, "A lot of friendships have been formed this week. I could see some of the women wanting to get together with others on a regular basis." Then she laughed. "After all, the eight of us formed our Bunco Club when we met at a retreat."

"And now look at all of you, you're practically inseparable."

"Yeah, but it's been a good thing," Marge said. "A *very* good thing for all of us."

"You bet it has. I'm happy for Phree that she has a tight-knit group of friends. You guys are just what my daughter needs."

Marge thought of Val and hoped she would also cultivate women friends. "As a woman there's nothing more satisfying than having the constant of good friends in your life."

"Well said," Sunnie noted. "Anyway, last night was like Mardi Gras around here. No one wanted to head to bed early or let go of the MQR experience. Let me just say the wine was flowing!" Sunnie made the universal hand signal for imbibing by sticking out a thumb and pinky from her fist while throwing her head back and 'drinking ' from her thumb. "And they especially loved Chef Evelyn's surprise midnight snack."

"I didn't know about this. Do tell." Marge dropped her chin in her hand, elbow on the desk.

"Do-it-yourself sundaes! She had everything prepared. All the fixin's were ready on a cart in the walk-in fridge. All I had to do was grab the tubs of flavored ice cream from the freezer and roll the whole shebang into the Brewster Quilting Room precisely at midnight. She even supplied some kind of sparkler type candles so the arrival of the ice cream looked like a fireworks display."

"We are so lucky to have her." Marge was smiling. "She's a genius."

"She's *our* genius," Sunnie added.

Shortly after noon things started to pop, and the disembarkment of passengers from the Mayflower Quilters Retreat was in full swing.

Ricky arrived and his legs never stopped churning as he transported countless items from the building to waiting vehicles in the parking lot. He had been the only male face the guests had seen on a regular basis and to a woman, they ALL loved Rick Mitchell. He had become an instant hit of the passengers…their very own rock star. Marge couldn't count the times she had been asked, "Will that nice young man be helping in the Mess Hall tonight?"

Marge, along with Nedra, Phree, and Sunnie, laughed, hugged, and schmoozed with the guests until one by one it was time to say goodbye. Quips were made in reference to leaving a ship and 'Ahoy, Captain' was used several times with Marge. Many eyes shone with unshed tears while others let them flow freely.

Marge held up fairly well under the rampant emotions until it was time to bid Heloise farewell. After embracing her most memorable guest, Marge walked her down the stairs of the porch with an arm around the woman's shoulders. They would part here, where reality ended and fantasy began, at the doorway of new friendships and unknown possibilities, a welcoming haven where quilters had the opportunity to revel in their sewing obsession for days.

Marge didn't mind that her cheeks were damp. "I'm going to miss you, lady."

"And I shall miss you, Marge Russell, GM of the Mayflower Quilters Retreat."

They stepped apart.

As Marge waved, Heloise called out, "Sail away Captain Russell, for others need you in far off places."

Chicken Harvest Chowder Soup

6-8 servings

1 C. chopped onion
1 C. chopped carrots
2 ½ C. potatoes (peeled and diced)
1 C. water
Chicken, cooked, cut/chopped (Add as much or as little as you like)*
2 T. chicken bouillon
2 cans corn (undrained)
4 T. butter
4 T. flour
3 C. milk
1 lb. Velveeta cheese

Combine veggies and water. Simmer 15 minutes.
Add chicken, bouillon, and undrained corn. Simmer 10 minutes.
In another pan melt butter. Add flour, milk, and cheese. Cook till smooth and thickens.
Add to other mixture and simmer on low heat.

*Author's Note:
I find that two good sized breasts work well. I also like the ease of using a rotisserie chicken from the grocery store, but if it's on the smaller side more than two breasts will probably be needed.

Karen is available for quilt guild talks, quilt shop talks, library talks, and book club discussions. She also offers a trunk show or bed-turning of her quilts. Contact her at **KarenDeWitt7@gmail.com** or by visiting her blog at **KarenDeWittAuthor.blogspot.com.**

Karen DeWitt is an avid quilter who holds an MFA in studio art. She is also a member of a Bunco Club that has been together for more than twenty years. Karen lives in the Chicago suburbs with her husband, and they have one adult son.

Made in the USA
San Bernardino, CA
04 May 2016